MW00413545

THE MYSTERY
OF THE
MISSING MESSAGE

Virginia Ann Work

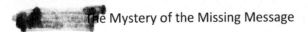

DEDICATION

To my three children:
Brian, Sherry and Vicki who inspired me to write
and who were my first readers of the Jodi series.
Thank you. You mean the world to me!

The Mystery of the Missing Message

The Mystery of the Missing Message

Prologue

This is weird! I never thought I'd write a book. But Mrs. Thompson, my English teacher, is helping me and everyone said I should do it. As you will see, I'm not a very experienced writer, but Mom says I have a gift for it and Mrs. Thompson agrees.

Now I'd better tell you about myself. My name is Jodi Elaine Fischer. I'm fifteen, and I live near Quesnel, British Columbia. My parents are missionaries to the Indian people, or First Nations people, as we say now. My family started out in Denver, Colorado. I don't usually like what I see when I look in a mirror, but they say I'm cute (not gorgeous!) with blue eyes, dimples and curly reddish-brown hair. The best thing about my life right now is my horse, Honey.

Oh. I forgot to tell you about my ten-year-old brother, Brian, who is the plague of my life, and my twin sisters, Bethany and Brittany, who are five – that cute but extremely annoying age.

My forever friend is Alexia Marguerita Marshal. We call her Lexie. She has long dark hair, a fantastic tan most of the year, and is the best student in her class. Her parents bought the big ranch house on the hill above our place as a (get this!) second home. Most of the year they live in Vancouver. Lexie's dad is a businessman and a politician. As soon as school is out, the Marshals come to Quesnel. They own several trophy-winning thoroughbred horses and show them around the province.

So this is my story. I've tried to start at the beginning and end at the ending and give a straight-forward account of everything in between. They say that's what a storyteller should do.

It all started last summer when Lexie and I found something surprising up in the woods while we were riding. Did I say surprising? Totally freaky is a better word! But I wasn't afraid at all. Ri--ght!

CHAPTER ONE

The Run-away

There was a sign where an old logging road forked into two dim trails. I pulled the reins and stopped to read it. This forest was home to me, for I'd spent most of my life exploring it, but I'd never before been up this way. The sun was warm on my bare head and I knew it would make my freckles stick out like the shiny fluorescent stickers I decorated my art work with.

"What do ya think?" I glanced at Lexie and read the sign out loud. "Private Road of Smith and Sons Logging Company, Limited. Not maintained. Travel at your own risk. Should we do it?"

Lexie shook her head and tucked her hair behind her ears. Her brow was furrowed as she squinted against the bright sun. "Let's go back. This is still our land, I think, but it looks spooky. Probably drug dealers are in there." She spoke to her horse, Cheyenne, who was pawing the ground. His coat shone like a bright copper penny and his black mane and tail were groomed to perfection. He was an expensive thoroughbred – I'd seen his papers – and trained for dressage and jumping.

I eyed the road. To me it looked mysterious and fun. What was down there? Why did the logging company feel it had to warn people away? "Ah, c'mon, Lexie. Live a little. If we don't go, we'll never know what was down there and we'd die, still wondering." I laughed at her worried expression.

A quick smile flashed across her face. "Okay. I guess I don't have anything to worry about as long as I'm with you." Pride was in the quick glance that she shot me. "You're the best rider in this area."

"Yeah, right. I doubt it. Best isn't good enough in most people's books."

Her face fell and she looked at me reproachfully.

I don't know why I always turn a compliment into a slam, but I do, and I felt sort of bad as I reined Honey into the little-used, rutted trail. Honey is a mixture of quarter horse and Morgan. I'd always loved palominos and now I had one. Dad said she had a nice combination of staying power and easy riding. But she didn't have the classic good looks of Cheyenne. I sighed. *Oh, well, she's mine and I'm grateful I have her.*

As I kicked Honey to a canter, I thought of the hours I'd spent on her, getting ready for the horse show coming up on the weekend. I'd be riding in the junior reining class and *maybe* I'd walk away with a trophy. But I almost missed going to it.

Mom and Dad were missionaries to the Indian people who lived on small reserves near our home. My folks were required to attend a conference of the missionaries once a year. I knew about the conference, but wasn't concerned about it as it was two weeks away. But last Sunday, just before dinner, Mom announced that we had to go *this* week instead, and that all us were going.

"But, Mom," I said, my voice rising to a howl, "you *know* I'm entered in the show and I've been working so *hard* ..."

"That's enough, young lady," Dad said, coming into the kitchen and snatching a warm cookie from the tray I'd pulled from the oven. "We know about your show, but the date for the conference was moved. We have to go and we aren't leaving you here by yourself. It's just too dangerous."

"Dangerous!" I slammed down the pan and rested my hands on my hips, anger rising to the surface. "I'm old enough to stay alone. And the Marshals said we could stay ..."

"The Marshals are busy folks," Mom said, tucking a strand of sandy-colored hair behind one ear, "and we aren't going to ask ..."

"But Lexie said I could stay with her whenever I needed to!" I blinked against the tears that threatened. "It isn't fair! I've worked so hard for this. I can't believe you'd be so mean to ..." I lifted the last cookie from the pan, threw down the spatula, and flew from the room.

"Jodi Elaine Fischer, come back here!" Dad's voice boomed down the hall but I slammed my bedroom door and flopped down on the bed. I picked up my cell phone and began texting Lexie furiously.

Suddenly the door opened. It was Mom. Her hair was frizzy around her face and her normally cheerful face was red. I could see frustration in her eyes. "Jodi, get out to the kitchen right now! And if you can be mature and not fly off the handle, we'll talk about it."

I didn't like the implication of the word *mature*, but hope sprang in my heart. I snapped my phone shut and stared at Mom, anger draining away like snow melting in the spring. "Meaning?"

Mom shrugged slightly. "Just what I said."

I followed her back to the kitchen. Dad was flipping hamburgers on the grill outside on the deck, so I loaded up with plates, silverware and glasses and went out. Mom followed with the potato salad and buns. Brian was outside already, playing kickball with the twins, Bethany and Brittany, on the back lawn.

Dad wiped his hands. He looked at me directly, his face dark. "I think you need to apologize, Jodi."

I sank down on the bench and sighed. "Okay. I'm sorry. I know you don't want to keep me away from the show on purpose. But I really want to show Honey." Again tears stung the backs of my eyelids. I stood and placed the settings carefully on the checkered tablecloth.

I could sense rather than see Mom and Dad eyeing one another like they do when they reach a decision without saying anything. How they do it is a mystery, but I've decided it must be one of those things that happen when you've lived with someone for so long.

Dad cleared his throat and put the hamburgers on a plate. "Well, I guess we can see if Mrs. Marshal wouldn't mind if you and Brian stayed with them. We can take the twins."

"Really?" It seemed like the sun suddenly came out from behind clouds and the world was bearable again. "You mean it?"

Dad grinned. "You have to promise to be good and do what they say and be nice to your brother."

"Yeah." I gazed out on the lawn where Brian caught the ball but fell while doing it. I laughed and brushed the tears from my eyes at the same time. "I can do that. At least I'll try."

Now, as a crow cawed up in a big pine, I pulled back on the reins and slowed Honey to a walk. Lexie, on Cheyenne, came up beside me. "Little pest," I said under my breath, thinking of Brian and the way he intruded on my life. He'd even wanted to come on this ride and we had to sneak off.

"What?" Lexie asked, pushing back her hair that flopped across her face.

I sniffed, enjoying the smell of pine and damp earth. "I just wish Mom and Dad had taken Brian with them to the conference. He's so ... he's such a brat sometimes!"

Lexie whirled to face me. "Jodi Fischer, I swear I don't understand you sometimes! I wish I had just one brother or sister and you have three!"

I could have kicked myself. I knew how badly Lexie wanted a brother or sister. She was the most sought-after babysitter in the whole neighborhood.

We rode on in silence. Except for an occasional bee buzzing by or a scolding squirrel, the woods were quiet. I swatted at a mosquito and glanced at my watch. At the next little clearing, I pulled Honey to a stop.

"Let's eat our lunch here." I swung down from Honey's back. Lexie dismounted, too, and we loosened the cinches of the saddles. I stretched and breathed deeply of leather and the warm, salty scent of horse. "Um," I murmured. "That's the best perfume in the world!"

Lexie laughed and fished the lunches from the saddle bags. "What is?"

"Horse smell, of course!" I flopped onto the grass and unwrapped my sandwich. "I think I'll bottle it and sell it to horse lovers. Probably make a million." I glanced over at Lexie, wishing I had her clear, smooth skin and her eyes and dark hair. It's a wonder she doesn't have to fight the boys off. But I knew she hardly ever dated.

"Remember when you moved in?" I bit into an apple. "I was so excited."

Lexie laughed. "Gosh, your eyes got bigger and bigger every time they unloaded one of our horses. I got excited when I saw you sitting there on Honey!"

"Yeah. It sure didn't take long to get to know you." I took another large bite of apple and thought about how Lexie had become a regular visitor in our house, how she loved to babysit the twins, how we spent hours messing around with the horses.

"You know," Lexie said thoughtfully, "at first I couldn't figure out what your dad did. To me a missionary was a weird person who wore funny clothes and preached all the time. Your dad sure doesn't fit *that* description."

"That was before you really knew us." I finished off the apple, wishing for a napkin, or a *serviette*, as they say in Canada. "I remember that time you came to our service on the reserve with the Indian people. You looked scared, like they were going to scalp you."

Lexie shot me an amused look. "No, I didn't think that." She grew thoughtful, munching on her apple. "But I didn't know what was going to happen. I didn't know anything about God. Not until you told me how to pray for Jesus to come into my life."

I remembered the night we talked in my bedroom until late. Her eyes were like saucers when I asked if she wanted to go to heaven or hell. Then she'd bowed her head and said a simple prayer. Wow. It sure changed everything about her. And I had a forever friend -- a Christian -- someone I could talk with about God and the Bible.

Suddenly I was startled from my thoughts by the report of a gun away off in the woods. *Who would be shooting this time of year?* I glanced around fearfully. "That's strange. No one should be hunting now."

"Maybe it's someone target practicing." Lexie gathered bits of plastic wrap and tucked them into the paper sack.

I ran my fingers through my hair and sighed. "No, there's no one around this time of year. It's scary." I paused and stared into the forest. "I'm so tired of being afraid all the time. I think I'm frightened of my own shadow."

Lexie stood. "You sure weren't afraid a couple of weeks ago at the rodeo. Anyone who'd ride into a corral with a Brahma bull *has* to be brave."

I shook my head. "You're right. I wasn't scared -- I was *terrified*. But when I saw that little girl fall into the show ring and the bull start to charge her, I knew I had to do something. And I was closest to the gate."

It's all a blur to me, even now – the anger that swept through me and made my fear disappear; the dust and smell of horse sweat; the eyes of the little girl lying on the ground. Even when I leapt from the saddle, grabbed the girl and remounted, it seemed a dream, like it was happening to someone else. The crowd cheered, Mom said, but I didn't hear them as I dug my heels into Honey's side and escaped the bull's charge by an eyelash.

And even though I'd been praised as a hero and had my picture in the paper, I knew that deep inside I was a coward. A real coward, because I'd been so scared throughout the whole ordeal that I couldn't think straight and had only acted from impulse. Surely brave people didn't feel like that!

I got up and stretched. "Well, let's go find out what's down this road, Lexie. Then I should be getting back. I'm starting to feel guilty about leaving Brian like we did."

Lexie nodded and tightened the cinch on her saddle. Then she put her foot in the stirrup. "Hey, what's this?" She removed her foot, leaned over and picked something up from the road. "It's a wallet! Look, Jodi!"

I hopped down from Honey and took it from her. "Let's see." I started to open it, but Lexie put her hand on my arm.

"Wait! Do you think we should? I mean, isn't it kind of a breach of privacy or something to look inside?"

I shook my head. "We have to. How else can we find out who owns it? But who would drop a wallet way out here in the middle of nowhere?" It felt thick. I drew a breath and opened it. We both gasped when we saw the wad bills in the back.

"Cool!" Lexie's voice was low. "How much is it?"

I stood there frozen for a second like an idiot when I saw all that dough. Crisp, multi-colored Canadian bills filled the bills compartment. Lexie was probably used to seeing stacks of money, but I wasn't. We hoarded pennies in our house and did without a lot of things.

"Okay, let's count it." I drew them out one by one and laid them in Lexie's hand.

" … ten hundred, eleven hundred, twelve hundred, thirteen hundred, fourteen hundred, fifteen hundred." I stopped and stared into Lexie's eyes. "You're holding fifteen hundred dollars, Lexie Marshal!"

Her face was as white as her t-shirt. "What are we going to do?" Hurriedly, almost as if the money burned her hand, she stuffed the bills back into the wallet. "We should take it to the RCMP. Now!"

The Royal Canadian Mounted Police is the police force in Canada, and they're called that because they used to ride horses. Most people shorten it to RCMP.

"I wonder if there's a name in here somewhere." I rooted through the other compartments. "Oh. Here it is. A driver's license. This belongs to Mr. Carl Sanders. He lives at 325 Walnut Drive in Vancouver. Wow." I closed it and stuffed it into a zippered pocket on my saddle. "Let's ride some more, then when we get back, we'll have your Mom drive us into Quesnel and drop it off at the RCMP office."

Lexie remounted, but her eyes were wary and she was not smiling. "I don't know. I'm afraid we'll lose it. Or something bad will happen. Maybe the guy who dropped it is over there, behind that tree, with a gun. I think we should go back *right now*." She gathered the reins and began turning Cheyenne.

"Oh, Lexie. We have time and there's nobody in the woods. C'mon." I urged Honey further down the road and glanced back, glad to see Lexie following, however grudgingly. Cheyenne seemed anxious to get the ride over with, because he plunged ahead and she had a hard time controlling him.

Just as I was relaxing back against the saddle, I spotted a movement on the ground. A squirrel darted out of the woods and jumped right between Cheyenne's slender legs. With a snort, the horse lunged forward. Lexie clutched the saddle horn as he leaped ahead and thundered down the road.

I dug my heels into Honey's sides. "C'mon, girl! We gotta keep up!"

Cheyenne kept the lead as the two horses raced down the road. At one point, the road split off again. I glimpsed a sign as I whizzed past. It had No. 043 painted on it in faded yellow letters. The road now was nothing more than a trail. Big holes appeared abruptly. A tiny stream crossed it.

Lexie and her frightened horse disappeared around a sharp bend. When Honey rounded it, I saw a fallen log across the road. Cheyenne was halted in front of it and Lexie was trying to regain her seat in the saddle. I pulled hard on the reins and Honey came to a sliding stop right beside the blood bay thoroughbred.

Cheyenne held his head low. His sides were heaving. Lexie fell out of the saddle and began patting him, talking to him in a soothing voice. I shook my head. If that had been *my* horse, I'd have been tempted to kick him in the rear!

I swung down. "Whew! That was some ride!"

"I'll say!" Lexie sank down on the log as if her legs couldn't hold her up any longer. Her usually well-groomed hair was out of its band and was in a tangled mess around her shoulders. "Where are we? I don't think I've ever been here before."

"I haven't a clue." I sat beside her, allowing Honey to blow. "I saw another sign back there that said this road was 043. I sure hope we can find our way back." I shivered. The sun had gone down behind the fringe of trees on the horizon and the woods were close and dark.

"I bet my cell phone doesn't have service." She drew it out, tried it and stuck it back in her pocket. "Nope. Hey, maybe we can build a fire and send smoke signals. Oh, well. Cheyenne will get us back. He likes his stall and oats so much, he'll find the way. I think."

Suddenly I saw something not far away in the woods. I stood and craned my neck, trying to see better.

"What're you looking at?"

"I'm not really sure, but, look! Right over there." I pointed. "Can you see anything?"

She stood beside me. "Is it the roof of a cabin?"

"That's what I thought, but I don't know. Do you think we should go see?"

She shrugged. "Why not? It's probably an old cabin the loggers threw up when they were working this part of the woods. It won't hurt anything to look at it." She gathered the reins and climbed on her horse.

I mounted Honey and directed her around the log. Soon we were back on the road. "There it is!" I pulled back on the reins while Lexie rode up beside me. Across a small clearing was a little log cabin. "Let's go see it!"

We tied the horses to a willow bush and stepped into the clearing. The old cabin stood bashfully to the rear of the clearing, next to the woods. Two black holes that were once windows stared out the front. An old door sagged open like a tired horse. The porch roof had partially collapsed and the steps were rotting away.

Slowly I led the way closer. And closer. "It … it looks sort of spooky." My voice was low, almost a whisper. Goosebumps raced up and down my back and my mouth felt like it was full of cotton. "Maybe this is as far as we should go."

"I don't believe in spooks." Lexie's voice was strong, but I heard a waver in it. "But it does … look … weird. Jodi, let's get out of here!"

I stepped up onto the rotting boards of the front porch and jumped when they screeched. She followed me closely – in fact, she clutched my t-shirt. A musty, damp odor filtered out through the windows and the open door. I crept up to one window and peered into the darkness.

At that very moment, a shuffling, heavy footstep made the old boards inside the cabin moan. I clenched her arm and looked into her eyes. Fear froze me to the spot, like I'd been planted there. *"What was that?"*

"I don't know."

Then it came again – a heavy footstep, and far back in the cabin, a board screeched.

She whirled and leaped off the porch. I was about to follow when something on the ground caught my eye. Something blue. I grabbed it up and stuffed it into my pocket.

Sprinting across the uneven grass and weeds, I followed her slender figure through the clearing. In one swift motion, we untied the horses, mounted, and were flying down the broken old road in the direction of home.

Or so we hoped.

After about a mile, my pulses returned to something like normal. I pulled on the reins, slowed Honey to a walk and leaned back in the saddle. Already the moon had risen in the evening sky and an owl hooted off in the woods. I let the air from my lungs and glanced at Lexie. "Someone was in that cabin."

"Yeah, I know." Her fingers on the reins were white.

I swallowed a lump in my throat. "That really scared me," I said slowly. I ran my fingers through my hair. "I've always been afraid. Of everything."

"Do you know why?"

"When I was four and Brian was about a year old, we lived on a small farm in Colorado. One night, I can still remember it as if it happened yesterday, Mom was getting the water ready to bathe Brian. Dad was out milking. All of a sudden – " I paused and rubbed down the bumps on my arms.

"What? What happened?"She reined Cheyenne closer.

"It was awful. These two men came into the house. They had nylon stockings over their faces and they carried guns. Mom just about fainted. Dad came in with the milk and spilled it all over the floor. I can remember thinking someone should mop it up. They wanted money. Dad gave them all we had, but it wasn't much. Then they were gone." I sighed. "But I still have nightmares about it."

I glanced up. We entered a large clearing. Ahead and up a hill, I saw the Marshal's big house, brightly lit. Nearer were the corrals and the barns. Off to the right, I could see the top of my home down in the hollow.

About that time a small white horse came into view down the lane; someone was riding at full tilt and I knew who it was, even though it was too dark to see his face. As he drew closer, I could make out the small white oval of his face beneath his huge cowboy hat. He sat securely in the saddle on his Welsh pony, Pepper.

"Let's not say anything about the cabin to Brian," I said quickly.

"Okay." Lexie agreed, but I heard disapproval in her voice. "By the way, what took you so long when we ran away from the cabin? I thought you were right behind me, but you weren't."

"Oh! I almost forgot. I found something on the ground just off the porch." From my pocket, I dug the soft thing I'd picked up from the ground.

"What is it?" She leaned over, trying to see in the dim light.

"I don't know." I spread it out on my palm. "Hey, it's … it's a knitted baby's sock*! A blue one!"*

CHAPTER TWO

A Knife in the Dark

She took the tiny sock in her hand. "Gosh! How did something like this get up there in the woods? It looks new." I reclaimed the hand-knitted footwear and tucked it away as Brian rode up.

"Where have you been so long?" he yelled, his blond hair falling into his eyes. He reined Pepper beside us.

"Cheyenne ran away up an old logging road." Lexie smiled at him and directed her horse toward the corral. "Did you have fun at Roger's?"

"Yeah," Brian replied. "But how come you guys always take off without me? It isn't fair. And you told Mom and Dad you'd include me in things, Jodi." His accusing blue eyes flashed in my direction.

I shrugged. "How am I supposed to include you when you go off to play with your friend? Don't be so stupid."

"I'm not stupid."

"Yes, you are."

"Am not."

"Am."

"All right, you two, cut it out!" Lexie threw a glance over her shoulder at us and dismounted at the corral. Brian turned Pepper away toward our house where he would put him out to pasture. He would

18

complain about the return walk, but I thought the exercise was good for him.

"You should try to get along with him," Lexie said in a low voice while we pulled the saddles off the horses. "Just think what you would do if anything should happen to him."

I frowned. "But he does stupid things all the time. Like the time he ruined my new cowboy hat by going in swimming with it." I lifted the saddle and carried it to the rack in the tack room. A twinge of guilt knocked on my heart. I sighed. "I guess I should be nicer to him, but he's such a pest! Oh, well, I was little once, too." I giggled. It sounded like something Mom would say.

The Marshal's barn was like everything else they owned – large, classy, and furnished with everything under the sun. I loved it. Mr. Marshal kept several valuable horses in roomy stalls. Overhead was the hay loft and to the sides of the long inner aisle were rooms for tack, a lounge, and equipment. Sedge, the Marshal's hired hand, kept the barn sparkling clean. He was sweeping the center aisle now, and looked up as we ducked into the tack room. He nodded and tipped the bill of his cap. "Evenin', Miss."

Lexie smiled and returned his nod. I wondered how it would be to have servants call me *Miss*.

After we hefted the saddles to their places and hung up the bridles, I admired the cabinet of trophies and ribbons that lined the walls. There was one whole wall dedicated to pictures of Mr. Marshal on several horses or in the show ring, holding their halters.

Toward the bottom of the long row, Lexie was pictured with Cheyenne. Both of them looked proud of the ribbon she held.

It was a different kind of horse world than the kind I knew. I was grateful for Honey and Pepper, but I'd never dreamt of showing them. Brian and I rode bareback through the woods, and in the summer, we rode to the creek and dove off their backs as they stood in the water. We'd even pile four or five little kids on Honey's back and she never complained.

But this summer Lexie begged me to train Honey for dressage and compete in horse shows. It was heaven. Her Mom promised to take us to the shows in their fancy pickup and horse trailer and my parents bought me a whole outfit -- helmet, black boots, white shirt and gloves! I was so excited. My first show was on Friday. It was going to be great.

I picked up a brush and went back outside. Grooming the horses took up a huge amount of our time. Honey was standing patiently at the rail fence, finishing her pan of oats. I started brushing her. "Maybe it was dropped by some picnickers."

Lexie stared at me over Cheyenne's back. "What? Oh – the sock. But we didn't see any car tracks. Besides, who would go way up there to have a picnic?"

"Hey! Maybe it's the person who dropped the wallet!" *Was he the man in the cabin? But why would he have a baby's sock?* It didn't make sense.

The house door banged shut and in a moment Mrs. Marshal joined us at the corral. She was a small, slender woman with short brown hair and sparkly hazel eyes. She was always dressed as if she was going to church, or to a concert. But I noticed she didn't smile much. *I wonder why. She has everything anyone could ever want! Or did she?*

"Hi, girls!" Her smile flitted across her face and was gone, almost as if it was too shy to be seen for long. "How did your ride go? Did you have trouble? You were gone a long time."

"Hi, Mom." Lexie continued to curry Cheyenne's coat until every speck of dust was gone. "I'm sorry we're late. Cheyenne spooked and bolted. I couldn't hold him."

"Spooked?" Mrs. Marshal was not acquainted with horse talk. "What do you mean?"

"He ran away, Mrs. Marshal." I finished Honey's grooming and turned with a smile. "A squirrel ran between his legs. Lexie hung on for dear life. It was fun."

"Fun!" Mrs. Marshal clutched her jacket closer around her chest and shuddered. "You have a strange sense of enjoyment, dear."

"It *was* fun, sorta," Lexie chimed in. "After I got done being scared out of my spit." I saw Mrs. Marshal frown, but I grinned. Lexie was starting to talk like us Fischers. "But, Mom, the most interesting thing is that we found a wallet. And it had, like, lots of money in it!"

Lexie's mom swung her head to us and stared. She squinted against the last rays of the sun as it sank behind the fringe of trees on the hill. "A wallet? Where? How much was in it?"

I suddenly remembered it was still in the pocket on my saddle. And that Sedge Murray had been sweeping the center aisle. "Oh, darn! I forgot! Hang on! It's in my saddle." I bolted to the tack room. *What if it's gone!* Panic made me almost breathless as I unzipped the pocket. *Whew!* It was still there. I felt the smooth, worn leather as I pulled it out and ran back to the corral.

Lexie had released the two horses into the pasture and was just finishing the story of finding it when I dashed up to them.

I held it up triumphantly. "It has fifteen hundred dollars in it, Mrs. Marshal! We counted!" Tingles of excitement flew down my back. I'd never had so much money before in my hand and it gave me a funny sense of power.

"Let me have it!" Mrs. Marshal held out her hand.

Reluctantly I handed it over. She looked inside, then slipped it into the pocket of her jacket. "I'm going to town tomorrow. You can come with me and turn this in to the RCMP. I'll keep it in our safe until then." She turned to leave, then glanced at Lexie. "You promised you'd make a cake for supper. Come on up as soon as you can."

"Okay." She tucked stray strands of hair behind her ears and watched Cheyenne roll in the dirt. After I gathered the brushes and put them up in the tack room, we went up to the house.

If Lexie showed me a new horse world, her parents introduced me to a different kind of living world. The house was big, with a wide covered deck that ran around three sides. The large windows glowed with lights. As I stepped in the front hallway, I shrugged out of my sweatshirt and took off my runners, which is what Canadians call tennis shoes. I should explain that everyone takes off their shoes at the door in Canada. Then I padded after Lexie.

Every room was full of expensive furniture and decorations – I never got tired of looking at all the nice stuff – and was kept immaculately clean. Its real oak floors, inset large screen TV in the den, marble counter tops, chandeliers, and gleaming appliances in the kitchen made me feel as if I was on movie set. I dusted off the seat of my jeans and ran my fingers through my hair, trying to fix it into some sort of order.

But it wouldn't fix. I passed a mirror and sighed. I hated my nose for being too short and turned up and I hated the freckles that sprinkled across it. Everyone said my large, blue eyes were my "redeeming feature" – I wondered what I needed redeeming from. Ugliness?

I went to the kitchen where I washed my hands at the sink. Lexie joined me and got out the mixing bowl, but Maria, the Marshal's live-in maid, had the cake almost finished. I liked Maria. She was an older Mexican lady, spoke good English with only a little accent, and was a cheerful presence in the kitchen.

"I didn't know when you would come home," she said to Lexie. "So I started cake. This is good?"

"Oh, yeah. Thanks, Maria. I'll do the rest." She poured the dough into a pan and shoved it into the oven.

"Can I do anything?" I felt like a fifth wheel on a four-wheel wagon.

Maria smiled at me. I think she liked me, too. "*Nada*. Have drink. Here, ma'am. Drink." She held out a crystal glass and a bottle of sparkling juice. I accepted it, wondering for just a split second before I raised it to my mouth if it was wine. But then I saw Lexie's grin and knew it wasn't.

Mrs. Marshal picked up her cell phone when it rang. From hearing the one-sided conversation, I figured it was Mr. Marshal and that he wouldn't be making it home for dinner.

When Traci Marshal snapped shut the phone, she shook her head and looked at Lexie. "I'm sorry, but Daddy won't be with us tonight. He can't get away from that meeting." She sighed. "So it will just be us, Maria. Take a setting off the table."

Deep inside, I relaxed a tiny bit. Somehow Mr. Marshal made me feel uneasy. He seemed so mysterious and solemn and everyone kind of tiptoed around him.

Brian came in a little while later. I took him quickly to one of the bathrooms to wash. I didn't know which towel to let him use – they all looked brand new. Finally I selected a small blue one. I tried to comb down his untamed blond hair but he wouldn't let me do much. When he was as presentable as I could make him, we joined the others just as Maria announced dinner.

As I pulled up the chair at the formal dining table and watched Maria bring in the food, a wave of loneliness swept over me. You might think I'm strange, but yes, I missed our crazy, noisy family -- the silly things the twins say and do, the dog barking, and even Brian spilling his milk. My dog, Sugar, was at the kennel. Dad said he wouldn't bother the Marshals with her.

I ate the soup politely and nudged Brian when he slurped. The old grandfather clock ticked loudly in the quiet house. Lexie seemed sad. I knew she missed her dad. After supper, we watched a movie and then got ready for bed. Brian went to one of the many guest rooms. I told him good night and said a prayer with him, like Dad did every night.

But I wasn't sleepy. Lexie was soon snoring, but I was wide awake as anything. Finally I went out onto the deck, carrying a blanket. I snuggled down on one of the padded lawn chairs and stared off into the woods. I don't know if I dozed, or what, but suddenly it was very dark.

A cold wind tossed the treetops and a wolf howled out in the woods somewhere. But danger was closer than that. I knew it, could feel it. My muscles froze and my legs and arms wouldn't work. Someone was coming! I inched forward, holding the leather wallet in my hands. I realized I was in the barn – I could smell the hay and hear the quiet cooing of the pigeons in the rafters.

Then I saw him. He was tall, broad-shouldered, dark-haired. He wore a hat – the kind they wear in old detective movies. He was coming toward me and I knew he wanted the wallet. But he must not get it! A shiver descended my spine. I tried to run and could only stumble down the aisle. His footsteps grew closer. I heard a low growl; it sounded like a dog growling, or a bear. But it was *him*.

I glanced over my shoulder as a ray of moonlight touched his face. *Mr. Marshal!* "Just give it to me, Jodi. You might as well not run because I've got men out there who are waiting for you. Hand it over."

And suddenly he wasn't Mr. Marshal. He was Colton, a guy from school. His long hair hid his face and he approached on cat's feet. "Give it over. I'll kill you if you don't give it to me." Then I saw he held a knife. He lifted it and thrust toward me. I screamed.

CHAPTER THREE

The Picture of A Crook

I lay on the wooden planks of the deck, the blanket tangled around me. The moon shone brightly on the lawn. It took me several seconds to remember where I was and that I'd just had a bad dream. I was cold. I returned to Lexie's room. She was asleep; moonlight played on her pretty face.

After I made a visit to the bathroom, I hopped into bed. But it took me a long while to get back to sleep.

The next morning, someone ripped off the covers and said something. I groaned and rolled over. But the annoying person wouldn't leave me alone. I stretched and looked up. It was Lexie. I noticed through my usual early morning blur that she was already dressed, had her makeup on, and was talking about the day.

"You better get up! Maria said she wouldn't keep breakfast warm for sleepy heads!" Lexie grinned. "*I* already had mine! *And* I fed the horses some grain and read my Bible!" She looked really good in her new white shorts and tan legs and her new top, the pink one with ruffled edges around the scooped neckline.

I groaned again. "Oh, go away. Do you want an award or something?" I pulled on my robe and found my slippers, feeling like a granny and moving like one, too.

She laughed and sat at her dressing table. She brushed out her long hair and swept it up into a pony tail. "Can I see that baby's sock we found yesterday?"

27

I grabbed my jeans from the chair near the bed and pulled it out. I handed it to Lexie and then scrambled into my clothes – a pair of dark blue shorts and a western cut blouse. We'd be going to town and I should look decent. I brushed my teeth and groaned inwardly as I tried to fix my hair into a semblance of order, but it bounced back from my comb like it had a mind of its own.

"Look, Jodi." Lexie turned on the bench in front of her dressing table. "There's something sewn or knitted right into this! It feels like a piece of paper."

I went over to her and stared at the bootie. "Can you get it out?"

"I think so – let's see …" She kneaded it with her fingers. The knitting was double thickness and between the two layers was a small piece of paper. By working it carefully, she was able to draw it out.

I took it from her hand before she could unfold it. After scanning it, I looked up. "It doesn't seem complete, and it sure doesn't make sense!"

"What does it say?"

I read it out loud. "We will ask … cash for the … we will find … to hide the … for a place … he will be your …" I turned the paper over, expecting more words, but it was blank.

"What does it mean?"

"I don't know." I sat down hard on the bed, my heart pounding heavily in my ears. It was a clue. I ran my fingers through my hair and scrunched up my eyes. But nothing helped. I couldn't figure it out.

Lexie came over and took it from me, studying it. "Hey, I know! I bet the words that would finish these sentences are in the other sock. The one that matches this. There has to be another one. Babies have two feet, you know." She was leaning over me, like she was going to press me into bed. Her eyes were dark and her hair swung down and brushed my face.

I had to laugh. I pushed her away and stood. "Well, then, I guess we have to go search that cabin and find it."

"Girls!" Mrs. Marshal's voice came down the hallway. "Let's go!"

"Oh, Mom's in a hurry. You'll have to grab a muffin, Jodi, and a glass of juice. C'mon." Lexie crammed the sock in her underwear drawer and led the way from the room.

Brian didn't mind staying home – he was enjoying the Marshal's plasma TV and the prospect of playing with Lexie's Wii. If he got bored, he said he'd take a dip in their pool. His tone was that of a too-rich spoiled brat.

It was my duty to bring him back to earth. "Not unless someone will watch you," I warned him, "that's the rule. And you have to walk home and feed the cats."

"I know. Maria will watch me if I want to swim. She said she has some knitting to do."

I stared at him, thinking of the knitted sock we'd found and wondering if … no, that was way too crazy. Why would Maria drop one of her knitting projects up in the woods? What would she be doing up there? "Okay, runt. Keep out of trouble." I patted his shoulder and winked.

Gray clouds hung low over the trees and the air was thick and muggy as we climbed in the car and drove into town. The mosquitoes were thick – even in town. It was a good-sized city in the center of the province that was built from gold mining and lumber. The Fraser River flows through the town and two big bridges span it. It boasts of a lumber mill, a hospital, schools and a busy downtown shopping area.

Mrs. Marshal parked downtown and gathered her purse when she got out of the car. She dug the wallet from her purse and handed it to Lexie. "I have some errands to run. Will you girls go right up to the RCMP office and turn this in?"

"Sure, Mom." Lexie tucked the wallet into her own purse and patted it. "Don't worry. We won't tell anyone we have fifteen hundred dollars in here!"

"Sh!" Mrs. Marshal glanced around nervously. There weren't too many people on the street, but she looked about as comfortable as a cat in a roomful of rocking chairs. "Just hurry and do it!"

"Boy, just think what we could buy with this!" Lexie whispered as we strode toward the police station.

I grabbed her elbow and squeezed. "Just stop talking about it! I feel like everyone is watching us!"

Having my head down and my eyes on the sidewalk, I didn't see what was coming, or I should say *who* was coming. Some guy cannoned right into me! I let out a little scream and tried to get away from him. All I could think of was that someone was going to snatch Lexie's purse … and the money.

I staggered, grabbed for something, and found myself clutching this guy's arm. Then I realized who it was. Colton! Colton Sommonichy … or whatever ... a name I couldn't ever pronounce. His long, lank hair hung over his face and he smelled like garbage and smoke and maybe beer. I couldn't believe it. I'd just had a dream about him!

He seemed as surprised as I was, but he sure recovered faster. Before I could even stammer out something, he said, "Jodi! Hey, babe! Am I ever glad to see *you!*"

He was still holding onto my arms. I brushed off his hands and stepped back. "Colton! What're you doing here?"

He looked up and down the street like he was guilty of something. Then he grinned. "What've you been up to this summer? I've been meanin' to come to your church services, but I've been busy."

I'd been glad when Colton came with some of his friends to our services, but I was suspicious of his motive. "I've been doing okay. You okay?"

He nodded and shoved his hands in his pockets and leaned closer to me. I could barely stand to be so near to him and I sensed Lexie edging away. He said, "I got a real good deal comin' down. Me and my friends, we're gonna clean up big, and then I'll be able to show you a good time. How 'bout that? I'll be big stuff in this town! And I'll come to your church all duded up in clothes that'll make your eyes pop. You wait and see."

I stepped back again. "My parents are away. I'm staying with my friend, Lexie, so we won't be having church this Sunday. Sorry."

"Well, that means you can go out with me. Wanta see a movie? Go dancin'?" He laughed. "Or are you not allowed to have a good time?"

"I'm … sorry, Colton, but I'm busy this week. See you." I managed to slip by him and join Lexie further down the street. "Thanks a bunch for abandoning me to … to that." My face was hot and my hands were cold. "That was awful."

She was real sympathetic. I could tell from her giggle. "It looked kinda funny. But I'm glad he didn't hit on me! I think I would've slapped him!"

This time *I* laughed. "I'd like to see that! But did you hear what he said? He wants to take me out! I can see it now in the paper – *Missionary Daughter Dates Town Drunk*!" I shook my head.

"What'd he say to you?"

"He said something about the fact that he had a big deal going down. And he'd be getting a lot of money soon." I shivered, repulsed by his touch. "But he said he couldn't tell me what it is. Sounds fishy to me."

"Well, he certainly looks the type to be involved in some crime." She didn't mean to, but sometimes she could sound so stuck up.

I didn't like Colton particularly, but I felt sorry for him. I knew that his folks had abandoned him when he was a little kid, and he'd been brought up in foster homes. Most of the time he hung out on the streets. What chance did he have? I couldn't imagine living like that. But on the other hand, I wasn't about to volunteer to be his girlfriend! How come the very guys I don't like hit on me and the ones I *do*, like Randy Abbot, don't know I exist? It wasn't fair.

Well, in the middle of these gloomy thoughts, we arrived at the RCMP office, a square building built of bricks. I hesitated at the door, suddenly almost overcome with dread. The fear I held at bay most times reared its ugly head. What if they suspected *me* of doing drugs? Or something worse? What if *I* was dragged into a web of crime and got arrested? How would it feel to spend the rest of my days behind bars?

"C'mon, Jodi!" Lexie held the door for me. She was grinning and her brown eyes sparkled with laughter. "These are the good guys, remember?"

I shook off the negative thoughts and stepped inside. A tall, young officer stood at a long counter near the door. A smile played on his lips as if he'd heard her comment.

"Can I help you?"

She dug the wallet from her purse and laid it on the counter like she was selling calendars or something. "Yes, you can. We found this wallet and want to turn it in. It has lots of money in it."

"Hmm." The officer glanced through the billfold. He called another officer, an older man, to come and witness as he counted the money. They filled out a form and signed it. Then they had us sign it. We also put down our addresses and phone number, in case, he said, someone didn't claim the money. Then it was ours.

When we were finished, he nodded as if he'd reached a decision. "You girls found something important, and I'm not talking about the money. Would you mind waiting for a moment? I'd like you to talk to someone else." He hurried off through a side door without receiving our permission.

I eyed Lexie. "I wonder what that's all about!" I could *feel* the handcuffs on my wrists and just knew they'd haul us off to a cell. But I didn't have much time to think about it, because the officer returned right away.

There was a glimmer in his eyes. "Would you girls mind stepping back here in this office for just a moment? We have some questions we'd like to ask you."

Lexie took a step backward. "Oh, but my mom – she's expecting us …"

"Do you have a cell phone? Could you call her and ask her to come up here? We'd like her to accompany you to the office."

"Oh, yeah." She drew out her phone and pressed the button. She spoke for a just a few moments. When she flipped it shut, she said, "She's shopping and said she could be here in about ten minutes. Is that okay?"

"Fine. Sit down and wait. I'll bring you some magazines." He delivered the magazines and went back behind the counter.

Traci Marshal appeared in fifteen minutes. She was out of breath and demanded to know what this was all about from the young officer at the counter. I heard her say in a strident voice, *"Do you know who I am?"*

I felt a little sorry for him when she demanded to talk to the sergeant. She was led to an office and reappeared in a more subdued frame of mind. I don't know what she was told, but she came meekly enough and sat beside us. She didn't say anything – only snatched up a fashion magazine and sunk her nose into it.

It wasn't long before the officer approached us warily. "I'm sorry for the delay. You can come this way, please." He ushered us behind the counter and down a short hallway to a small, plain room. In its center stood a table with four wooden straight-backed chairs around it. I half expected to see a strobe light in the ceiling and instruments of torture arranged on the counter by the wall.

Mrs. Marshal chose a chair that was shoved back into a corner of the room. She crossed her long, shapely legs, and continued to read the magazine that she'd brought along. I was amazed she wasn't concerned at all about the proceedings, but then realized she'd seen a lot more of life than I had.

"Office, my eye!" I whispered indignantly to Lexie. I refused to sit on the chair. Maybe they were electrified. "I bet this is one of those rooms where they sweat the truth from criminals!"

She laughed, plunked down on a chair, and set her purse on the table. "Jodi, you're a hoot. You have enough imagination for ten people. Just sit down and try not to be so silly!"

There – I heard that stuck-up tone in her voice again. It grated on my nerves.

The door opened. A smiling, broad-shouldered man stepped in and closed the door. I felt trapped when he shut the door, but there wasn't anything I could do about it. He was wearing a dark suit, a white shirt and a red tie. And dress shoes.

He nodded to Mrs. Marshal. "Hello, I'm Detective Walters." He held out his hand. She lowered the magazine long enough to shake his hand, but you could tell by the way she did it, with just her fingers, and not even a smile on her face, that she considered him below her notice.

He switched his attention to us. "I'll be looking into your case, girls." His eyes brightened when he glanced at me. "You can have a seat, Miss Fischer."

I nodded and perched on the edge of the chair, twisting my fingers together in my lap. "How do you know my name?"

His smile widened. "I occasionally look in the paper and I remember seeing your face in it just recently. Saved a little girl, didn't you? That was a brave thing to do."

I felt a wave of heat warm my neck and face. In spite of myself, I found I liked him. "Well, I did it because I *had* to. But what do you mean about a *case*? I didn't know we had one."

He laughed and glanced at Lexie, as if she was somehow in on the joke. "Oh, but you do. And you, young lady, must be Alexia Marshal."

She extended a hand. "Just Lexie, please. Nice to meet you, Detective."

He shook her hand, then brought out a sheaf of papers. "I'd like to get your story straight. I don't think you're criminals, so you can relax." He looked pointedly at me and smiled again. "If you'd just fill out this form and write in as much detail as you can about

when and how you found the wallet, I'd appreciate it."
He handed us both a form and a pen. Then he stood.
"Would you like something to drink? A Coke?"

"Yeah, that would be great." I pulled the chair
closer to the table.

"Make mine a Sprite." She'd already started with
her form, printing neatly.

He asked Mrs. Marshal if she'd like coffee, but she
shook her head without lifting her eyes.

I could only hope that I didn't mess up my form – I
was so nervous I couldn't even remember my address!
But I managed to get through it and we finished about
the same time. Mr. Walters brought the pop and when
we'd finished writing, he read over what we'd written.

"You say you found the wallet on a logging road
up in the woods beyond your place, but I need to know
where exactly." He tapped the form with his pen.

I shrugged. "How can we tell you? There's no
address. We'd have to show you."

He nodded. "Okay. How about today? Can you
take me up there now?" He glanced at Mrs. Marshal.
"What are your plans, Mrs. Marshal?"

She lowered the magazine a fraction of an inch and
glared at him. "I have more shopping to do, and an
appointment. We're busy people, officer. I'd have to
check my schedule and get back with you."

"But, Mom! *We* don't want to shop!" Lexie picked
up her purse and stood. "We could go with him now,
and he could drop us off at the house when we're
finished."

Mr. Walters shuffled the papers into a briefcase. "I
can ask one of the female constables to come with us,

if that would make you feel better, ma'am." His tone was extremely differential, but I noticed his brow was furrowed and his eyes flashed.

She considered it while she folded the magazine and got to her feet. Then she nodded. "Very well." She walked beside Lexie as we went out. "I'll see you at home," she said to Lexie. "If you have any problems, call me." She hesitated and pulled her to a stop. "You don't have to put up with any hasseling. Remember that."

Lexie rolled her eyes and sighed, shrugging away from her mom's grip. "I know, Mom. See you later."

I was curious to see the female officer, imagining her to be one of those masculine-type women with short, cropped hair and shoulders the size of a football player's and a voice like a logger. But the women who appeared had mousy-brown hair, didn't talk much, and smiled shyly at me as if she was afraid I'd bite her.

"Megan Peters," she said and nodded. We murmured the appropriate response and went out into the muggy, overcast day. I think Mr. Walters said something about the weather, but Megan didn't say anything at all. She was in a RCMP uniform, the brown one, but she looked smart in it, not masculine at all.

Mr. Walters opened the front door of the police car. Megan removed her hat and climbed in the front seat. I realized that Lexie wasn't with us and thought maybe she had to get something from her mom's car. But she emerged from the office and after a quick glance around, flew over to the squad car. She and I climbed in the back.

"What were you doing?" I asked in a whisper as we snapped on our seat belts.

She flashed me a look that said she was excited about something. "Tell you later."

On the way home, I fought down an uneasy feeling that started in the pit of my stomach and worked its way upward to my head. This was too weird for words. Why were the police so interested in an old wallet? How did it tie in with the cabin? Or did it?

For the first part of the trip, we followed the famous Fraser River, the one the gold miners traveled to find gold a hundred years ago. It seemed unbelievable that just a few miles away, in Barkerville, millions of dollars of gold had been taken from the earth. What a change since then! Now the gold was being taken from the tourist's pockets.

We left the river and climbed to a high plateau. We passed small ranches, little creeks wandering through meadows, birch and aspen trees framing the darker forests of pines and firs, and ramshackle ranch houses beside decrepit barns.

We arrived at the Marshal's house and Lexie directed Mr. Walters to the small road that led past the barn. It was my job to open and shut the gates.

"Which way?" Mr. Walters paused as the road forked.

"To the left," I said. I glanced at Lexie. "I hope we can remember where we stopped for lunch."

"So do I."

The car bounced over pot holes and crept over streams that had encroached on the road. "Here!" I said as a small clearing came into view. Mr. Walter slammed on the brakes. "This is where we ate lunch. I'm sure of it."

We all got out. The detective began looking all around, closely inspecting the road and the bushes. Megan followed him with a camera in her hand.

"Just exactly where did you find the wallet?" He straightened and glanced my way.

I swatted a mosquito. It was so hard to tell exactly, but finally I found the spot where we'd gotten on the horses. "I think it was right around here. Why's it so important?"

He ignored my question and examined the ground, hunched over, not quite kneeling. Lexie and I stood to one side, as he'd asked us not to disturb the area too much. After staring at the ground for what seemed an eternity, he motioned for us to come closer.

"See this?" His finger traced a footprint in the dust. "This is too large for either of you, a man's shoe. I bet this is the man who lost the wallet. Looks like he stopped his vehicle, got out and then got back in. Lucky I could find it. You and your horses nearly erased it."

"What do you want that for?" I leaned closer, trying to see the faint print.

"Well, we'll get a picture of it. We can also fill it with plaster and make a copy. I have the equipment in the car. Just part of my work." He straightened and smiled.

We watched, fascinated, as the two constables took pictures and a plaster cast of the footprint. It was dry in a matter of minutes. Mr. Walters seemed pleased with it. They labeled it and signed an envelope. Megan also found a cigarette butt in the bushes that they put in an envelope. It was just like a CSI episode, which I'd seen only a couple of times, since Mom and Dad said it was too gruesome for us kids.

When they finished, Mr. Walters motioned on down the road. "Where does this lead? Is this your land?"

Lexie nodded. "I think so, but you'd have to ask my dad. I don't know where it goes. Just an old logging road. We only rode about a mile down it and found a cabin."

His eyes brightened and he stopped dusting off his hands. "A cabin? Hm. That might be interesting. I'll have to come back and do some exploring. But not in this rig. Okay, let's go."

"You can leave us off at the house," Lexie said in her most grown-up voice.

He nodded and we started bouncing back to the corral. As we drew closer to the house, my curiosity got the better of me. "Mr. Walters, I was wondering something."

"Yes?" He glanced in the rear view mirror.

"Well, why are you looking for clues and everything? What's going on?"

He didn't answer until he'd stopped by the big house. He turned to us just before we climbed out. "I'm sorry, Jodi, but I can't tell you. But I'd like to have your help. If you hear or see anything strange, please call me, okay? Here's my card." He handed each of us a card with his name and cell phone number on it.

"Sure." I accepted the card. Lexie nodded in agreement and tucked it in her purse.

We got out of the police car and waved as he drove off.

"Jodi!" Lexie grabbed my arm.

"What!" She about scared my socks off, if I'd been wearing socks, which I wasn't.

"I think I know." Her face, only inches from mine, looked like a ghost's or a vampire's. I had the weird thought that maybe she *was* a vampire!

I shrugged off the thought and giggled. "Know what?"

"I think I know why Mr. Walters was looking for clues and stuff. On my way out of the police station, I happened to see some wanted posters hanging on a bulletin board by the door. I glanced at them. One name hit me. It was Joe – let's see – Joe somebody." She rubbed her forehead and I wanted to shake her. "He was wanted for armed robbery and kidnapping. And guess what! One of his aliases, you know fake names, was Carl Sanders!"

I know my eyes were like saucers and it felt like someone ran cold fingers down my back. "Carl Sanders! That's the name in the wallet! Lexie, that means a wanted criminal is right here in *our woods*!"

CHAPTER FOUR

A Big Mess

Well, they aren't *my* woods, but you know what I mean.

We put our coats in the closet and took off our shoes. Next we went to the bedroom and changed clothes. I could tell the thought of real criminals so close to the house bothered Lexie. She kept her eyes lowered and was quiet for awhile. Then she got out the sock and sat on her bed, looking at it.

"Do you think we should have told him about this – and the note?"

"I don't know. I guess we should tell him everything, but I kinda wanted something to ... check out, investigate, by ourselves. Maybe that was wrong."

"Well, we can call him." She tucked it back in her drawer. "Let's go see what Maria has for lunch. I kinda suggested quesadillas, so I hope she made them. Mom will be home soon."

I had a queasy feeling in the pit of my stomach as we helped Maria put the finishing touches on lunch – pouring the iced tea and setting the little table in the small dining room off the kitchen. The trees came close to the house in the back, and I couldn't help but gaze out the window and wonder if someone was out there, watching us. I wondered if they knew we had the sock.

We waited past noon for Mrs. Marshal. Finally she called Lexie. When she put down the phone, her eyes were troubled. "Mom says she got to her appointment late and then ran into a friend, and they're going out for lunch. Then she has *another* appointment this afternoon."

Brian came charging through the door just as we prayed. He took off his cowboy boots at the front door and then charged into the informal dining room off the kitchen, bringing the smell of horses and hay with him.

"Go wash, cowboy," I told him, pointing him to the bathroom. "We don't take dirty cowpokes at this dude ranch."

The quesadillas were mouth-watering wonderful. Brian was full of his adventures when he came back. I tried to motion to him not to eat and talk at the same time, but he missed my cues entirely.

"Boy! Did me and Roger have fun! We pretended we were detectives and we rode up in the woods." He gulped his lemonade and didn't bother to wipe his mouth. "This police car came by on the road and looked us over real good. Then we rode up further and spied on these two men. They were talking together, like maybe they had drugs or something, and then they got in their truck and drove off."

Lexie shot me a quick glance. "Where were you in the woods?"

He waved his hand vaguely. "Oh, just right up there. Not too far from the swimming hole." He brushed his blond hair from his eyes and attacked another quesadilla.

I gave him what I hoped was a grown-up look for, *straighten up and don't be such a pig*, then said, "What did the men look like? And their truck?"

"I dunno. It was beat up. Used to be yellow. Covered with dirt. An older model Chevy, I think. Cracked windshield. And the men..." He paused, staring off into space. "I'd say they were not too old. Both wore kind of sloppy, dirty clothes. Had hats on, so I couldn't see their faces. One was tall and kind of skinny. Why?"

Lexie laid down her fork carefully. "Oh, gosh. That's really scary."

"Whatd'ya mean, scary? It was a blast." He slurped his drink and wiped his face with a sleeve.

She raised her eyebrows. "Jodi, we're gonna have to tell him."

Brian yanked on my arm. "Tell me what? Hey, what's going on? You gotta let me in on it or I'm gonna tell Mom how you guys took off on your ride without me."

I wiped my mouth and let the air from my lungs with a swoosh. "Shut up! And quit being so ..." I paused and caught a look from Lexie. "Okay. We can't tell you now. Just be patient and when we're finished, we'll meet you down at the barn. Okay?"

"Great." He finished a piece of cake in three mouthfuls and dashed outside. But not before he thanked Maria for the delicious lunch. I patted his arm as he ran past and gave him a smile.

We helped Maria clean up the kitchen. I was wiping off the counter when Brian burst in the back door from the deck. He was breathing hard. Something had scared him bad. "Hey, you guys! Something's happened down at the barn!"

I whirled around and caught his shoulders. He wasn't joking. His face was pale with shock and he was trembling. "What happened?"

"The tack room!" He waved his hands around. I had to dodge his gestures. "You ought to see it! It's a mess!"

"It's *what*?" Lexie almost dropped the dish she was putting away. "We always leave it neat. Sedge wouldn't let us go without cleaning up."

He headed out the door again, hollering over his shoulder, "C'mon! I'll show you!"

"Go ... go, now! Shoo!" Maria waved us away from the kitchen good-naturedly, as if this were all kid's play, a joke.

"Thanks for the lunch!" I yelled as I leaped from the deck just behind Brian. We raced down to the barn, through the big double doors and down the center aisle. I didn't see Sedge Murray anywhere around. Lexie was ahead of me and stopped suddenly at the door of the tack room, her hand on her mouth.

"Oh gosh."

I shoved past her. It *was* a mess! All the ointments, bandages and other medicines that had been neatly stored on the shelves were in a heap on the floor. Boxes of buckles, clamps, chains, leather straps, along with the grooming tools – brushes, picks, curry combs – were lying in the center of the room. And riding on top of it all was an assortment of saddles, bridles and ropes.

Lexie was moaning under her breath, sifting through the pile like she was looking for lost treasure. "Who would have done this – and why?"

"Yeah, why," Brian echoed. "I'm sure glad I don't have to clean this up!"

Lexie regarded him seriously, wiping her hands on her shorts. "Well, we can't do this alone. It'd be great if you'd help."

"Me?" He took a step backward and sighed. "Okay. Where do I start?"

"No, wait!" I held up my hand. "Somebody did this for a reason. If we look, we may find some kind of a clue that will tell us who did it and why."

"Lexie!" Mrs. Marshal called from the house.

Lexie grabbed my arm with a pincer grip. "Rats! I didn't think Mom would be getting back so soon. I have to go. We can't let her see this. She'd worry her head off and make us stop riding. This'll have to wait. C'mon!"

"Okay," I said slowly, "but listen. I'll stay here. Brian, you go get your camera. We'll get some shots of this before we clean it up. Then we can show the pictures to Mr. Walters."

"Who's Mr. Walters?" Brian moved to the door.

Lexie nodded. "I have a camera. I think it's better than his. You can take videos with it. Come on, Brian. We'll tell you later." She steered him out of the barn.

I poked around a bit at the heap of equipment while he was gone, but I didn't want to disturb anything too much. Soon he was back, puffing from the run, Lexie's digital camera swinging from his hand.

"Here. Mrs. Marshal came and she's going out again. She sure goes a lot!"

I nodded absently and took some pictures, making sure the lighting was okay. I took about three minutes of video, panning the room slowly. We moved to the light in the center aisle and studied the pictures and the video. They all came out clearly. I was proud of my detective efforts!

"I'll take the camera back to the house and you go get Sedge. He lives in that trailer over there." I pointed in the general direction of his trailer house that was set on the edge of the corral. "It'll take all four of us to get this mess back in order."

"Aye, aye, *moi capitaine*," he said, saluting. He'd been watching too many old movies, combining them with his French lessons which were required in Canada.

I took the camera to the house and Lexie returned with me to the barn. Brian and Mr. Murray had just arrived.

Sedge shook his head sorrowfully. He was an older man who kept to himself and seemed to need little, except to be around horses. I liked him. "This is a big mess, no joke." He was from some other country, but had been in Canada for most of his life. "I will sleep out here and catch next guy who wants to do this!" His face was red as he shook his fist into the air.

I almost laughed, but caught myself in time. He looked so comical with his gray, straggly hair sticking out all over from his head. But suddenly I felt sorry for him. Poor old guy. This was his whole world, and he was extremely neat. It must have seemed like the end of everything to him.

It was hot and sticky. We worked steadily for about an hour and all I could think of was the pool. We had the job almost finished when Lexie threw her hand over her mouth.

"Oh, darn! I forgot! I was supposed to call Mrs. Anderson about that babysitting job tomorrow night! And my phone's up at the house. See you in a few." She bolted out the door.

Mr. Murray lifted his head from the pile of jumbled buckles, rings and clamps he was sorting. "You kids can go now. Go call police, yah? Maybe they catch the guy who did this. Thank you for your help."

I patted his shoulder, told him not to work too hard, and together with Brian, started up the hill to the house.

"I sure have a lot of questions," Brian complained as we stepped into the kitchen where a roast was sending out delicious smells from the oven and cookies cooled on the counter.

Lexie came in. "I just called and canceled. Too much going on right now. Mrs. Anderson said she can get someone else. Hey. Let's take a swim and then we can answer all of Brian's questions."

I nodded. "Sounds like a plan, but I'd better call Mr. Walters before we do anything else." I found the card he'd given me and on the second ring, he picked up.

"I'm so glad I got you!" I said, my voice rising with emotion. "Something's happened that's really scary!"

His voice was low and calm. "Just take a breath and tell me as clearly as you can everything that happened, Jodi." Somehow that settled me down.

"A couple of hours ago, I don't know, I guess it was around two, we found that someone had come into the Marshal's barn and messed up the tack room. Turned it upside-down. Everything was dumped into the middle of the room. Honest! We got Mr. Murray ..."

"Who's that?"

"Oh. The caretaker of the grounds and barn. He's an older man. He talks funny, like he's a foreigner or something. Anyway, he helped us clean it up. I took some pictures. Can you come out?"

"Sorry, I can't make it today, but I'll be out tomorrow morning. Do the Marshals want to file a complaint?"

"I don't know. They aren't home. And Lexie doesn't want to tell her mom. She's afraid she'll worry too much."

He cleared his throat. "Well, if I come out, I'll need to talk to her about it. And to Mr. Marshal, too, if he's home." He sounded in a hurry, or distracted, or something. "See you then. Keep this under wraps, okay, Jodi? We don't want the whole countryside knowing about it."

"Okay. Thanks. Bye." But he was already gone. I snapped shut my phone and went to the bedroom.

Lexie and I changed into our swimsuits and joined Brian at the pool.

"Would someone tell me what's going on?" he asked pleadingly after we dove in and splashed around some.

I grinned and sent a spray of water in his direction. "Okay." Then we told him – Lexie and I – interrupting each other, but getting it all said in the end.

He wiped his face and bobbed in the shallow end. "Wow. Just think, we've got a real mystery right here in our own backyard! What would Mom and Dad say?"

I gulped at the thought. "They'd probably come straight home and tell us to let the police take care of it!"

"If they believed us," he said, swimming to the deep end and back again.

Lexie swept back her hair after a dive. "Hey, we have those pictures! I want to see them again. Jodi, would you mind going and getting the camera? Maybe later on we can print them out on my computer." She hefted herself from the pool and grabbed her towel.

"Sure." I clambered from the water and dried off quickly. "Let's do it right now before dinner!"

I padded into the house, careful not to leave wet footprints, and found the camera. Suddenly something moved just outside the open window. The lacy white stirred in the breeze, but there had been something out there on the deck. I stepped to the window and gazed out. But nothing was there. *Must have been my imagination.* But I knew it wasn't.

Was someone watching the house? Had they searched the tack room for the sock and the note? Had they seen us taking pictures, so came up to the house, bold as you please, to steal them from Lexie's room? I shivered and shut the window.

Quickly I got back into my clothes and sat on the bed, trying to control the pounding of my heart. *Why does everything have to be so scary?* Mr. Walters didn't seem to take this very seriously or he would have sent an officer out right away. *Oh, God! Please help me! I don't want to be like this!*

I picked up Lexie's Living Bible. On the inside of the front cover, she'd pasted a list of her favorite verses. On the top of the list was Psalm 56:3, "But when I am afraid, I will put my confidence in You. Yes, I will trust the promises of God. And since I am trusting Him, what can mere man do to me?"

A knock came on the door. I jumped. "Come in!"

Brian stuck his head in. "I thought you were getting the camera!"

"I am. I mean I was. Guess I got sidetracked."

Lexie came in and Brian left. She changed into her clothes and then led the way to the office. With Brian peering over our shoulders, we printed the pictures off her laptop. Then we studied them silently, one by one. After a few minutes, Brian picked up one of them.

"Hey, look at this! Whose is that?" He pointed to a jacket that was tossed on a bench by the wall.

"A jacket!" Lexie took the picture. "It *does* look like a coat. And look! Here it is in another picture."

"But whose is it?" I slid the picture from her fingers. It was a plaid jacket, red and black, lightweight, like you'd wear on a cool summer evening. It looked like a man's. "And who would be wearing it on a hot day like today?"

"It doesn't look like any of ours." Lexie rubbed her forehead.

"Maybe it's Mr. Murray's," I said with a little chuckle. "But I can't imagine him owning something like this." I glanced up. "Brian, why don't you run over to his trailer, show him the picture and ask him?"

He wasn't gone long. "Nope!" He threw himself down on the couch in the office. "He said, 'Who would wear a coat on a hot day?' Something like that."

I stood and paced to the window, staring out into the dark forest. The sun was down below the horizon and the mourning doves cooed in the bushes. Slowly I paced from the window to the desk and back to the window. "But when we went to clean up, the jacket wasn't there. Did anyone see it?"

They stared at me and shook their heads. I sat down suddenly; my knees felt weak. The front door slammed shut. We all jumped, but it was only Mrs. Marshal. About that time, Maria called us for dinner.

On the way down the hall, I whispered to Lexie, "So that means someone got it when we were all gone! Someone's watching us! I knew it!"

Lexie put a finger to her lips. "*Sh!* Don't say anything to my parents. I'll have to tell them, but not now." She straightened her shirt and brushed off her shorts.

Mr. Marshal arrived home about the time we got to the dining room. He washed his hands and joined us. After greeting one another in a rather formal way, we sat down. There was a white linen tablecloth on the table and sparkling silverware. Real silver, I figured. I hoped Brian wouldn't slurp his water or spill his gravy on the white carpet.

Mr. Marshal seemed in an expansive, positive mood. Not jolly. Just sort of talkative. He patted Mrs. Marshal's hand and grinned at the things she'd say, almost like they were courting or something. Or maybe he was going to surprise her somehow. But how could you surprise someone who has everything?

Anyway, dinner went by swiftly. Maria served coffee for the adults and a special punch she'd stirred up for us. Mr. Marshal excused himself and said he had some work to do in his office. Traci relaxed in front of the TV with a magazine and a third cup of coffee. She was quite pretty, in a made-up, fancy sort of way. She'd put on a pair of white shorts and a nice top. I sniffed. It just wasn't fair, having money and looks and everything.

We joined Traci in the family room. Brian settled in an easy chair with a book. The evening news came on. I picked up a book, but watched the news, as well.

The third story after we'd turned on the TV was from Vancouver. The reporter stood on a residential street. Lexie straightened. "Look, Mom! That's our street!"

"Tragedy struck this morning in this quiet residential area of Vancouver," the reporter was saying. "Matthew Salisbury, the infant child of Mr. and Mrs. Lloyd Salisbury, one of Vancouver's leading families, was abducted from their home early this morning. The Salisburys found a note in his crib, stating that they must pay one million dollars in ransom for their child. The note warned that they may never see their little boy alive again if they do not comply with the demand." The camera panned the large estate house of the Salisburys.

They inserted an interview with the distraught parents, asking for help to find their son. I studied the woman's tear-stained face, trying to imagine how it would feel to lose your child that way.

The reporter continued, "Anyone with information concerning this child is asked to contact the police immediately." They showed a picture of a little baby boy, probably no older than six months.

"Oh my!" Mrs. Marshal half rose, then sank down on the easy chair, her face the color of putty. "That's *awful!*"

Lexie glanced at me. "We know them. Mom and Dad belong to the same country club and play golf with them. And they live just down the street from us."She leaned forward and whispered, "I feel sorry for Mom! She's taken care of Matthew and just loves him!"

Traci called her husband to the room and told him about the tragedy. "One million dollars! Can they get that much together?"

"I don't know," Mr. Marshal shrugged. "But I'm glad it's not me in that kind of a predicament." He turned and went back to his office.

Lexie got up and motioned for me to follow her. "Dad?" she said softly at his door. "Can we talk to you?"

He looked up from his computer, distracted and a little put out. "What is it?"

"I thought you should know what's been going on around here." She walked into the room and I followed shyly. She told him about the things that had been happening, nodding to me several times to back up her statements.

"I don't know what to say about the ... what did you say? ... a baby's sock? whatever it was that you found in the woods. But this deal about the tack room, I think it's pranksters." He ran his fingers through his hair and sighed. "I don't need this right now. How can I take care of this kind of thing and my business, too?"

She touched his shoulder. "We already called the police, Dad. An inspector, Mr. Walters, is coming out tomorrow to run a routine check. Sedge said he'd check to see if anything's missing. But otherwise, it will depend on you whether you want to file a complaint or not."

He turned back to the screen and began typing. "Not if it's just kids. Tell the constable to contact me if he finds anything serious."

"Should we ask if they'd send someone out here to check on things regularly?" Lexie edged to the door. I was already there.

He glanced at her as if she'd saved his soul. "Yeah. That sounds like a good idea. Request that for me, will you, honey? Don't worry about things. It will be okay." He was gone again in his computer and we crept from the room.

That night I settled into bed after Lexie turned off the light. I'd begged her to leave a night light on and she had, but it didn't seem enough. The window was open. I wanted it closed but she refused on that one – it was so hot and muggy, we slept with no covers and still sweat made our pajamas stick to our skin.

I closed my eyes and tried to get to sleep, but all I could think of was a blue baby sock, a note, a messed up tack room and Colton's leering face. *Colton!* I sat upright in bed.

"Lexie!"

"Umm?"

"I just had a thought."

"Um."

"No, I mean it. Listen." I turned on the lamp. "I started thinking about what Colton said about cleaning up on a big deal. And the news tonight about the Salisbury's baby being kidnapped and I thought about that sock. A *blue sock!* I bet the kidnappers have the Salisbury baby in that old cabin up in the woods!"

.

CHAPTER FIVE

A Baby Arrives

Lexie jerked upright. "You're kidding!"

"I just remembered something else, too." I jumped up and got the note from her drawer. "These words! Listen to them again. 'We will ask … ask for the … We will find … to hide the … for a place … He will be your …'"

She shook her head, like she was trying to clear it of cobwebs. "It sure sounds like it might be a kidnapping plot."

"I think we should copy the words, just in case Mr. Walters want this." I grabbed a pen and a scrap of paper and quickly wrote them down. I stuffed the original note back into the drawer and collapsed on the bed.

The next morning Mr. Marshal was in a hurry to leave for his office in Quesnel. "Oh, Lexie," he called from the door. "I talked to Detective Walters. He said he was coming out today. I requested a regular check and he said they'd provide one. I told him I wouldn't be home, but that you and Jodi can show him around."

"Will do, Dad." Lexie popped around the corner.

"And he mentioned something about a cabin up in the woods. Said he might go up there. Would you tell him that I checked and found that the land and the cabin are owned by Smith and Sons Logging, Limited?"

"Sure." She lingered by his side and I could tell she wanted more attention from him, but he turned quickly to Traci who'd come up to the door. He kissed her good-bye and left.

Mrs. Marshal turned to Lexie after the door shut. "What in the world was *that* all about?"

She edged away. "Oh, it's really nothing, Mom." She led the way to the kitchen where Maria was scrambling eggs. The toast popped up and she began buttering it. "Yesterday some pranksters got in the barn and messed up the tack room a little. We called the police but even they didn't take it seriously. They want to come out today and look around."

"I'd say *that's* something!" Traci stood with her hands on her hips and her eyes blazing angrily. "How come I'm the last one to know about these things?" She stomped to the dining room and scooped up the newspaper that was on the table by her plate.

It was already hot by the time Mr. Walters drove up in his dark blue car. We were sitting on the front deck on the swing, reading. Brian was playing Wii inside, but he came bursting out of the house as soon as the inspector opened his car door.

"He's here!" Lexie stood. "Do you have the pictures, Jodi?"

I help up a white envelope that I'd been using for a book marker. "Right in here."

Mr. Walters came around the car and mounted the steps to the deck. He was carrying a black briefcase, and was dressed in a short-sleeved shirt and light colored slacks. No gun, as far as I could see. "Good morning, girls. And who is this?" He smiled at Brian.

"This is my little brother, Brian," I said. Brian shook his hand.

Traci approached from across the lawn where she'd been practicing her tennis shots at the court. She shook his hand soberly. "I hope you catch whoever did it," she said with a little pucker of her brow.

Mr. Walters shrugged. "Well, we don't have a lot to go on. I'm afraid we can only do a check. Now, I'll take a look at the barn and the room, if you kids would be good enough to show me around."

She excused herself, saying she had to get ready to go to town.

We walked with him to the barn and showed him around.

"Well," he said, pacing around in the tack room, "everything looks in order now. Too bad you had to clean it. There might have been some fingerprints."

I grunted. "You don't know Sedge Murray. He couldn't stand a mess in here very long. But we did take a few pictures before we straightened things up. Would you like to see them?"

"Yes, I would." He finished his inspection and followed us to the house, where we sat in lawn chairs on the back lawn. Lexie brought out the pictures. After thumbing through them, he looked at me with a funny expression. "Were any of you wearing a jacket yesterday? I noticed one in the pictures, but didn't see any hanging up down there."

I shook my head and leaned forward, tapping the picture. "None of us wore a jacket. It was too hot. We asked Sedge and he said it wasn't his, either. So that means …"

"Someone came back," he said, rubbing his chin, "and picked it up between when you took the pictures and when you cleaned up the room. Hm. Interesting."

Maria brought out some lemonade, a tall frosty glass for each of us, and a plate of cookies. The tray was even decorated with a spray of flowers.

He still held the pictures. "May I have these? We can enlarge them and take a closer look at the coat." He received his glass and took a drink. "Thanks."

"Sure," Lexie said. She crossed her leg over her knee and sipped her juice, looking like her mother.

Mr. Walters finished his drink and looked like he was getting ready to go.

"Before you go," I said, setting down my drink with a clunk on the paving at my feet, "there's more that you should know." I proceeded to tell him about what we found at the cabin and Lexie produced the sock and the note.

"It looks like you have a real mystery here," he said, studying them carefully. "I'll have to take these, I'm afraid. For evidence." He produced an envelope from his briefcase and put the note and sock in it, signed it and had us sign it, too. I was more than sorry to see it go, but glad I'd written down the words.

"It sounds like a kidnapping!" Brian said. I frowned at him, but he didn't catch on. "And last night on the news, they said that someone in Vancouver had their baby stolen. I bet they have that baby up there at the cabin!"

"Whoa, cowboy!" Mr. Walters held up his hand. "The first lesson a junior detective has to learn is not to jump to conclusions. We hardly have enough evidence to suggest that is the case. I have to admit, though, I'm curious as to what this means. And why it was in a baby sock. Strange." He straightened. "Well, let's go have a look at that cabin, shall we?"

"You mean we get to come with you?" Brian nearly leaped out of his skin.

"I don't see why not, if one of you will ask Mrs. Marshal for permission. I'm sort of off duty today."

Lexie ran inside. I suddenly remembered something. "Mr. Marshal said this morning that he checked his maps and he's pretty sure the cabin is owned by the logging company up there … Smith and Sons Logging, something like that."

Mr. Walters nodded. "I know. I checked, too. I called their office before I came out and they said it was vacant. And that I had their permission to search it if no one's in it."

Lexie returned. "She said it's okay. Let's go!"

I saw the smile Mr. Walters hid behind his hand as we climbed into his car. Just as we turned the corner by the barn, I glimpsed a movement in the woods. What was that? The horses? But the horses were in the pasture down by the creek. Was I imagining things again? Or had I really seen a shadow melt into the dark forest?

I shook off the uneasy feeling and relaxed against the leather seat. The air conditioning felt nice, but he switched it off and we opened our windows. We started up the old logging road and passed the sign.

The road narrowed to a bumpy trail. Suddenly the car swerved. I thought Mr. Walters was trying to miss a stump or something, but then felt a heavy *bump! bump! bump!* beneath me. The car stopped.

Mr. Walters groaned. "I bet we have a flat. Everyone out!"

Sure enough, the right front tire looked like a pancake. We swatted mosquitoes and fetched tools for Mr. Walters. The back of his nice clean shirt was soaked with sweat by the time he finished and we all wished we'd brought some water.

"Whew! I wonder what the temperature is!" He started the car and looked at the digital reading on the dash. "Ninety-nine! With this humidity it feels like a hundred and ten!" He turned up all the windows and started the air conditioner. It sure felt good.

But it was taking too long. *Hurry!* I wanted to yell it at Mr. Walters, but he seemed so unconcerned. My legs felt like ants were crawling up and down them. I longed to jump out and run. He eased the car over the ditches and the little stream of water like he was driving something made from pure gold. I glanced at Lexie and she raised her brows.

Finally we came to the place where the log blocked the road. It was gone.

Mr. Walters got out and examined it. "Someone's been using a chain saw," he said. I heard tension in his voice. When he got back in the car, he brought a revolver from the glove compartment and laid it on the seat beside him. "I'm not going to park close to the cabin. I want you to stay in the car, no matter what happens. Is that clear?" He glanced around at us and pierced each one of us with a stern glance.

"Yes, sir." We all said together.

Then he started off again, this time even slower.

I gulped, hard. I wasn't having fun anymore. Fear raised its ugly head and told me what a fool I was to get involved with something like this. I tried to push it away, but it remained niggling at the back of my brain like a naughty child.

It was his tone of voice when he gave that last instruction that sent shivers down my spine. After that, we were all very quiet. I grabbed Lexie's hand and squeezed it. Brian glanced at me from the front seat, his eyes wide and his face damp with sweat.

Mr. Walters pulled into the clearing in front of the cabin and parked behind a screen of bushes. I saw immediately that someone had mended the sagging door and put plastic on the empty windows. It looked like the grass had been trampled down – I saw tire tracks, but there was no vehicle. Had they gotten away? As slow as we'd been going, a whole *army* could've gotten away! I clenched my teeth and blinked hard against the stinging in my eyes.

Oh, God, watch over us right now. I'm sorry for all the mean things I've said to Brian. And the way I've not minded Mom and Dad. Please be with us right now. My fingers hurt; I was hanging onto the arm rest so hard. Suddenly, I heard a voice in my head. It was a voice I knew and loved, and it was quoting the verse I'd read. *But when I am afraid, I will put my confidence in You.*

Okay, Lord. But You've gotta help me on this one. I can't do it alone.

Mr. Walters strolled across the clearing like a tourist who'd lost his way, looking this way and that, whistling softly to himself. He climbed the porch and knocked loudly on the door. Hunched down on the seat, I glanced at Lexie and tried a smile, but it was a lame one. She returned it and squeezed my hand again.

"Hey! If he needs the gun, I'll run it over to him!" Brian whispered from the front seat, motioning to the revolver.

"Stop, silly!" I hissed at him.

About that time, a woman appeared at the door. She was slender and not too old – maybe around twenty-five. Her blond hair was drawn back into a pony tail. She wore jean shorts and a skimpy top that was cut low and pretty much showed off her you-know-whats. She eyed Mr. Walters for a few seconds and then glanced at the car. I could hear her clear voice; she sounded annoyed.

"Yes? May I help you?"

He said something so softly I couldn't hear.

"I don't know who you're talking about. I've never heard of them. You're way off the road, mister. Nobody lives up this way. Me and my man, we're with the logging company and we got permission to camp out here for a couple of days. He's off fishing. We got written permission. D'ya want to see it?" She stepped back, like she'd go get it.

"No, no. That's okay. I must have taken the wrong turn back there. I'm sure they said this road, though. We're meeting our friends for a picnic. Sorry to bother you, ma'am." He tipped his head, then came to the car. She closed the door.

"Well!" He turned the ignition, put on his seat belt and backed up. I saw the plastic move slightly at one of the windows just as we drove out of the clearing. "That's that."

"Can't you search the cabin or the clearing?" I leaned forward, willing him to stop, to look around, to find some clues.

He merely shook his head. "I don't think I'd find anything right now. Besides, we can't flush the bird too soon." He glanced at me in the mirror and winked.

At the house, we told him good-bye and he asked us again to notify him if we saw anything weird. As if we wouldn't! Lexie flopped down on her bed with a disappointed groan.

"Oh, man. I was hoping so hard that he'd find something and solve this!"

I paced the room, uneasy and afraid. The curtains swayed in the breeze and I thought again how easy it would be for someone to break into the house and search our things. "Well, like he says, we can't flush the bird too soon." We exchanged an amused glance. "But I know what you mean. I was so scared when we were at the cabin, I thought I'd *die!* It's fun reading about mysteries, but being in one is a different story."

She straightened and picked the lint from her bedspread. "We're not supposed to be afraid all the time. It sort of ... freezes you up ... you can't really live when you're afraid. It's like that verse I was reading this morning. It goes sorta like, God hasn't given us the spirit of fear but He has given us power, love and a sound mind." She got up and looked at the rifle her dad had given her for her birthday. It was a twenty-two caliber and she used it mainly to target practice. She took it down from its rack on the wall and loaded it. Then she grinned at me. "But it doesn't hurt to be prepared."

"Just watch where you point that thing." I don't like guns, but I'd gone out several times with her and shot the twenty-two. That was fun. "But how do you make that verse practical? I mean, when you're truly scared."

She shrugged and with a clean cloth, rubbed the barrel of the gun until it shone. "You just have to trust God. You shouldn't think about all the things that *could* happen. Concentrate on the good things that He has given us right now."

I smiled. Her faith was so simple and complete. She was always teaching me things. "Yeah, I guess you're right." I stretched. This inactivity was getting me down. "Hey, you wanta go for a ride? I bet we have time before dinner."

"Yeah, and maybe we can practice some dressage for the show. It's coming. Saturday, Jodi! Can you believe?" Her eyes sparkled at the thought. She returned the rifle to its rack.

I threw my hand over my mouth. "Oh darn! I forgot! Let's go practice, for sure. Honey needs a *lot* more work." This was Thursday. Saturday was almost here.

We spent the next two hours with the horses and I relaxed, as I always do, when I'm riding. I rode bareback, enjoying the feel of her. Sometimes it seemed like we were one creature. It was here, on Honey, that I felt the most secure and happy. What would I do if anything happened to her? I shook my head and pushed the thought away.

We had a good time, yet when I looked under the branches of the tall firs that surrounded the corral, into the dark and secret byways of the forest, I felt the old fear creeping back. *I will trust God. I will trust God.* Even as I directed Honey into the complicated steps of dressage, I repeated it over and over. It helped. A little.

We unsaddled and groomed the horses, then carried the saddles and tack to the barn. Honey had to roll, of course. Once in a while she could roll clear over. I'd heard that a horse that can do that is worth a hundred bucks per roll.

As we walked back up the house, I noticed a big motor home was parked at the back on the pad. It was one of those that you can expand out a room and looked like it cost about as much as our whole house had! Lexie didn't know who owned it.

We washed up and then stomped down the hallway to the kitchen to see what was for dinner.

"We have guests, Lexie," Traci Marshal met us halfway with a funny look on her face, something between disgust and anger. Two men were standing in the foyer, the cathedral entrance at the big double front doors. Traci led us there and stopped, as if unsure how to proceed.

Beside Mr. Marshal stood a shorter man who had a black beard and a large stomach. They were discussing something seriously, but turned when we approached.

Traci did the introduction. "Girls, this is Mr. Marshal's cousin, Mr. Clark. This is my daughter, Lexie, and her friend, Jodi Fischer."

I nodded to him in greeting and Lexie extended her hand. "Glad to meet you," she said.

He smiled. I involuntarily took a step back. His smile was worse than his sober face, which was enough to scare anybody. Brian burst in the door, just come from feeding the cats at our place. He slid to a stop. Traci mumbled his name. I exchanged glances with Brian, for I sensed he had the same reaction that I did to the stranger.

Mr. Clark swung his gaze to include all of us, then he smirked at Mr. Marshal. "What are you starting here, Dick? An orphanage?"

"No," Mr. Marshal ushered him away, toward his study. "They're visiting while their parents are away. Let's go in here. We can talk better." He glanced back. "Maria? I'd like some of that Cabernet wine, please. Two glasses."

"Yes, sir." Maria answered. She'd come out to take Mr. Clark's jacket.

"Who is *that*, Mom? I didn't know Dad had a cousin." Lexie followed her to the kitchen and perched on a bar stool at the breakfast bar. I hesitated in the doorway.

Traci shook her head and got a glass of wine for herself when Maria poured the other two. "I don't know." She sounded tired. "I guess they haven't seen each other for a long time and they were coming through, so stopped in."

I excused myself to go get some clean clothes on. I felt grubby in my jeans and t-shirt and with company, dinner would be extra formal. At home, the horse smell and a little dirt wouldn't have bothered anyone.

About half-way back down the hall, I stopped dead in my tracks. A tall woman emerged from one of the bedrooms. It wasn't that she was extraordinarily pretty or even nicely dressed. In fact, I didn't notice her clothes. It was what she was carrying that brought my heart to my throat.

In her arms, she held a baby about six months old – a boy and he was wearing a *blue knitted sweater!*

CHAPTER SIX

A Warning

After a quick change to a short denim skirt and a tank top, I returned to the kitchen. Lexie was holding the baby, who smiled up at her with dimples on each cheek.

"Look, Jodi! This is Mark. Isn't he adorable?"

I smoothed Mark's curly blond hair and laughed at the way he kicked his heels and squirmed on her lap. For only six months, this guy was a charmer. "He's cute! How old is he?"

Mrs. Clark turned from the sink where she'd washed out some bottles. "Six and a half months," she replied. She was wearing a black tailored suit, like business women wore to work, and a pendant of what looked like a real diamond. Her dark hair was piled on her head and her diamond-studded ear-rings flashed in the light. She didn't strike me as a motherly type woman. A constant half-frown played on her narrow face, and she avoided the direct gaze of people.

I glanced around to see if I could spot the sweater Mark was wearing, but it was gone. What had they done with it? Mr. Marshal found an old high chair in the garage and brought it in. Mrs. Clark placed the baby in it, even though he didn't eat much "real" food yet. She gave him some crackers and a few Cheerios.

71

He had fun with the crackers, smushing them all over his face.

During dinner, I watched the visitors. Why did they make me feel uneasy and suspicious? I decided by the time dessert was served that it was because Mr. Clark had that ridiculous beard that made him look like Blackbeard and because neither of them seemed very happy. I began to wonder if they weren't playing a part. But why?

Afterward, Lexie and I went outside and played croquette with Brian. It was still warm, and we had to put bug spray on our arms and legs to keep off the mosquitoes.

"Isn't Mark just adorable?" Lexie gushed as she tapped the ball through the hoop. "Oh, man. I wish he was ours."

"Yeah." It was my turn and I hit the ball way beyond the wicket. "It's too bad …"

"Too bad, what?" Lexie lifted her eyes and watched Brian smack the ball.

"Well, something doesn't seem right about them." I sighed. "I don't know. I guess my imagination –"

"I noticed it, too," Brian put in. He wiped sweat from his face and went to knock his ball back toward the hoop. "Something's wrong, but I can't put my finger on it."

Lexie stared at us with her hands on her hips. "Oh, you guys! You see a mystery everywhere, but you're wrong this time. There's nothing funny about them. They're just busy people. Mark's adorable and I won't have you saying anything bad about his folks!"

Well. That shut us up good and proper!

We played the round (Lexie won, as usual) and then collapsed on the swing. Maria brought out orange and raspberry slushies for us. Sweet Maria! How could we survive without her?

I just about choked on mine, though, as a thought brought me upright. "Hey! Doesn't it seem strange to you that we have *two* babies? *Two* little boys about six months old? *Two* blue knitted sweater and sock sets?"

Lexie set down her glass and wipe her mouth with a serviette. "Jodi, Mr. Walter said we shouldn't jump …"

"I know! I know what he's said!" I exclaimed. "But this is too big of a coincidence and it's strong evidence, too. What if …" I stared at Lexie, unable to say the words.

Brian said them for me. "Hey! What if Mark is the kidnapped baby? The Salisbury baby?"

Lexie had just taken another drink. She gasped and choked on her drink. When she recovered, she shook her head. "That is absolutely the most ridiculous thing I've ever heard!" We were all quiet for awhile. "Do you think he is? Seriously?"

I shrugged. "I don't know."

We finished our drink and went to the family room, but there was nothing good to watch on TV. I suggested a movie, but nothing seemed to interest us. Brian trotted off to watch something on TV is his room.

"Come here," I said to Lexie and led the way through her sliding glass doors to the deck, then around the deck, close to where the Clark's motor home was parked. I lowered my voice to a whisper.

"There's only one way to find out if Mark is the kidnapped baby or not. We have to find the other sock. If we find it in there," I motioned with my head to the motor home, "and there's a note in it, like we found in the other one, then we have proof. And we could solve this and get Mark, or Matthew, whichever he is, back to his parents."

Her eyes widened. "But how …"

"We have to get in there and look around."

"Oh, but, Jodi! We can't do that!" She took a step backward and put up her hands like she was warding off an attack. "That's … I don't know what they call it, but it's not right."

"Breaking and entering." I sighed. Of course it wasn't right. But it seemed like all we could do. "Well, let's just go and ask to see the inside, like we're curious. And maybe we can see it lying around. We could give it a try." Now that I'd latched onto the idea, I couldn't give it up. It seemed so logical. And the stakes … well, the stakes were pretty high. We could save that little boy from …

"Okay." Lexie took a deep breath and let it out slowly. "We can go ask, although I'll feel stupid if we are wrong."

We jumped down off the deck and circled the motor home. It was so big! And fancy! I felt a little overwhelmed when I climbed the steps and tapped on the door. *Nothing.* I thought Mrs. Clark said she was going to put Mark to bed. But maybe they'd gotten to talking and she hadn't done it yet.

I knocked the second time and glanced at Lexie. Her eyes, usually large and round, seemed like saucers. The sun was just setting behind the fringe of trees on the hill and I heard a cow mooing for its baby.

"Come on, Jodi, they aren't home." Lexie turned.

"Wait."

She rotated her body and fixed me with a puzzled frown. "What are you going to do?"

"I … I can't let this go. What if we're right, Lexie? We'd be turning our backs on him. I don't think they'd mind if we just stepped inside and looked around a bit. Why would they, if they don't have anything to hide?"

She shook her head and crossed her arms on her chest. "All right, Jodi. You lead the way. But if we get caught …"

The door wasn't locked. I edged it open. "At least it isn't breaking and entering if they leave it unlocked," I whispered, as if *that* would make it better if we were caught.

We stepped inside. Just inside. The home was fabulous – I could tell it was the best of the best. And neat. No little blue sweater and sock lying about. A magazine on the table. A pair of shoes by the door. A baseball cap by the driver's seat. A couple of books beside the couch.

"You stay here and I'll look in the bedroom and bathroom," I whispered.

She nodded. "Just hurry!"

I went to the bedroom and on the queen-sized bed, was the diaper bag. I rummaged in it and pulled out the blue sweater. "Here it is! Look, Lexie!" I took it to her.

She felt it. "But does it match? The color doesn't seem quite the same. Too bad we gave that sock to Mr. Walters! Were there any other socks in the bag?"

"I don't know. I just found this and …" *Footsteps on the gravel!* And we hadn't even heard a door slamming at the house! *Low voices!* I ran back and stuffed the sweater in the bag. Lexie grabbed the door knob and turned, but it was yanked out of her hand.

Mr. Clark stood on the steps with his wife behind him, holding the baby. They both stared at us in surprise, their shock turning quickly to anger. I could see a red flush creeping up Mr. Clark's neck and his eyes narrowed like he was squinting. His wife gasped and stepped back.

"What are you doing, you –" He swore softly.

We tumbled out and past them.

He clutched my arm. "What's going on here? Just what are you two playing at?" When he wanted to be, he was fearsome. And he wanted to be right now.

I was so scared I couldn't talk. Almost wet my pants! But Lexie jumped in, cool as a cucumber.

She pulled me gently from his grasp and smiled. "Oh, we're so sorry, Mr. Clark! We wanted to see your beautiful home so much and you weren't around so we figured it wouldn't hurt to step inside and glance around. I'm so glad you came and I got to meet your adorable little boy! He's so sweet!"

She actually got Mark to smile – and he'd been fussing when they walked up.

"Yeah, we're sorry, sir," I chimed in, rubbing my arm. "We just looked around. Curious. We're *so* sorry. It was rude, wasn't it?"

My admission and Mark's giggle seemed to calm him down. He shook his head and muttered something about *stupid kids*. Mrs. Clark put her nose in the air and sniffed loudly. "*Rude* doesn't begin to describe it! It is our home and you need to ask if you go in someone's home."

We apologized again. And again. By the third time, Mark was fussy and they stomped into the motor home without a backward glance, both of them with stiff spines.

We retreated to Lexie's room and flopped down on our beds, none the wiser for our adventure. "Oh, that was awful," I moaned after a long, strained silence.

She rearranged the bottles on her dressing table and picked up her stuffed teddy bear, holding it close to her chest. "Well, I don't see why he got so mad. Unless –"

I nodded. "Unless he *does* have something to hide. But I feel ... I don't know, so guilty! Do you think he'll tell your dad?" I knew if *my* dad got a whiff of this, I'd be grounded for a month! Maybe for life!

She paced to the window, still holding the bear like he'd protect her. "I don't think so. It wasn't really bad. I mean, it was, but we apologized and everything."

I stood. "I don't agree with you." She glanced at me, surprise in her eyes. I went to the door. "What we did was wrong. We jumped to a conclusion, which Mr. Walters said not to do. Then we took matters in our own hands without asking anyone. And we shouldn't have gone into their home without being uninvited. Three strikes and you're out. That pretty much covers it."

She whirled away from me, but I could see a flush creeping onto her face. "If that's how you're going to be, then …"

I shrugged. "I don't see it any other way. I'm going for a walk." I didn't slam the door. I wasn't mad at Lexie; I was mad at myself.

The walk calmed me down a bit, but I hurried back because a big storm was rolling in over the hills. Thunder rumbled in the distance and I saw the occasional flash of lightning. I sure didn't want to be caught out in a storm! I checked on Honey and Cheyenne and they seemed to be okay, huddled next to the barn under the eaves. I opened the barn door and let them in the center aisle. Nothing in there that they could harm and they'd be more protected from the lightning.

Back at the house, everything seemed quiet. I found Lexie reading a book on the back porch. I apologized to her and we prayed together. We even went so far as to vow not to rush ahead with things like that again. *Fat chance!*

She said their guests and her mom and dad had decided to go into town to see a show, an Old Wild West show one of the pubs downtown put on every evening. Lexie was babysitting Mark – she checked on him every once in a while.

With a little twinkle in her eye, she said, "I took a good look at the sweater in the light and I think it's a different color than the sock we found. And there weren't any socks in the diaper bag, or anywhere, that I could see."

I nodded. "I sure wish we hadn't given it to Mr. Walters!"

Brian was still in his room, watching TV. I wandered out to the large living room, the one with the grand piano and stone fireplace. Such a big empty house! And they were hardly ever there to live in it.

Suddenly the phone rang. It startled me because I didn't know they had a land line. I'd only seen them with cell phones. It rang twice and I located it – in the kitchen. Maria must have gone to her apartment on the second floor because she wasn't in the kitchen.

On the third ring, I wondered if I should answer it. Or should I get Lexie. But there wasn't time. Gingerly, I picked up the receiver and said hello.

A man's voice, low and gruff, answered. "Who is this?"

I hesitated, taken aback. Finally I said, "Uh, Jodi Fischer. But you've reached the home of Mr. and Mrs. Marshal. Do you want to talk to them?"

"No. My message is for *you*." He breathed heavily into the phone.

"Who's this?" Panic surged through my system, freezing my muscles and making my mouth go dry. I swallowed. "Who *is* this?" I hoped it was just some kid from the neighborhood, playing a prank.

"Wouldn't you like to know, you snoopy little brat. Listen, kid, you better forget you ever saw a cabin. You know what I mean. And keep your cop friends away. You don't know what you're playing with. It would be pretty easy to put a bullet through your horse's head. And your friend's horse, too. In fact, I have them in my sights right now."

"But …"

"No buts about it. You heard me and I ain't going to repeat myself." The line went dead with a *click!*

My head was in a whirl, but even in my fear, I realized he was watching the house – he must be in the barn or near it. He'd seen the Marshals and Clarks leave. He knew we were alone. What would stop him from coming and …

A streak of lightning and a rumble of thunder crashed pretty close to the house. I jumped and screamed. The lights went out and came back on. Lexie ran into the kitchen, just as I dashed out. We collided. Then clung to each other, yelling our lungs out. Brian appeared next and looked at us like we were idiots.

He sniffed. "What's going on? It's just a lightning storm. C'mon, let's watch it from the deck."

"What about Mark? I hope he's okay." I disentangled myself from Lexie and straightened my clothes.

She threw her hand to her mouth and dashed out the side door to the deck. I could hear her running along it and hoped another bolt of lightning wouldn't – *boom!*

This time the lightning and thunder came at once, shaking the timbers of the house. The lights went out, and they stayed out. Brian stumbled off to get his flashlight and I tried to find a candle and some matches in the kitchen drawers.

Lexie reappeared with Mark in her arms. He was crying and rubbing his eyes. Brian came back with his flashlight.

"Look, Mark! Look at the light!" He swung the light around.

Mark stopped crying. Lexie bounced him on her hip. She actually looked more like a real mother than that Mrs. Clark had. I asked about candles and she showed me where they were. Mark loved the candles and tried to touch the light. We laughed and gave him a cookie. His big blue eyes sparkled in the light. I guess he thought it was real special to be up at this hour of the night and to be the center of attention.

Fifteen minutes later, the lights came on again. By that time the storm was moving off down the valley. We heated some water and had hot chocolate and cookies. Mark got sleepy and Lexie went to put him back to bed.

When she returned, we sat at the small table off the kitchen. She brought out a Phase 10 game.

I sipped my cocoa. The storm had been scary, but what had happened *before* the storm had frightened me worse. I ran my fingers through my hair. "Before we play, I want to tell you what happened just before the storm." Somehow with all the excitement of the storm and the lights going out and Mark needing attention, I'd forgotten it. They stopped shuffling the cards and looked at me.

"What? What happened now?" Lexie looked tired and I thought how much energy she'd put into taking care of Mark.

"I got a phone call. It was a man. He wouldn't say his name. It came on the house phone." I proceeded to tell them. Neither of them knew what to say.

Finally, Lexie said, "We should call Mr. Walters. He should know what to do. But I don't want my dad knowing. If he knew about this, he'd move the horses away."

"But … but what if they actually …" I couldn't go on.

"They won't," Brian said. "It's just a threat. C'mon, let's play."

CHAPTER SEVEN

Followed

The next morning strong sunlight streamed in the window and landed right in my eyes. I tried rolling over, but I smelled sausages frying in the kitchen. *What day is it?* I rubbed my eyes and tried to focus on the calendar on the wall. *Friday!* Tomorrow was the horse show!

I sat straight up in bed, suddenly wide awake. "Lexie! Get up!" I jumped out of bed and scrambled into my jeans and t-shirt. It wasn't so hot, thanks to the storm, but it was still humid. Muggy.

Lexie groaned. I pulled the sheet off her and made a face. "Look! I've already dressed and put my make-up on and had breakfast while you lazed in bed! I even had my devotions and fed the horses!"

"Did not!" She stuck her tongue out at me, but then laughed. "You little liar! You don't even *wear* make-up!"

"I do, too. Sometimes." I put on an injured air as she padded to the bathroom. She dressed in jean shorts and a t-shirt that read *Jesus is the King of my Heart.*

While we ate breakfast, Maria had the small flat screen TV in the kitchen turned to the news. Brian came in just as the newscaster said, "The baby of Mr. and Mrs. Salisbury, kidnapped last Thursday from his home in Vancouver, is still missing, police reported today. The Salisburys received a notice from the kidnappers through a newspaper ad, stating that they had until Sunday, August 15th to deliver the money. Other details of the kidnapping are being withheld. The strike that …"

"Sunday!" I turned to Lexie. "That's only two days!"

Lexie nodded soberly and continued eating, as if she didn't care at all. But of course I knew she did.

Lexie's mom and dad offered to take the Clarks around the country to see homes. I guess they were thinking of buying property in the area. Traci asked Lexie if she would mind watching Mark while they were gone.

"Sure!" Lexie beamed, holding out her arms for the little boy.

"We should be back by lunchtime, but I'll call."

Mrs. Clark left instructions for Mark, then hurried off to get her purse.

I was wishing that I'd paid closer attention to the news broadcast when we first saw it, because they'd shown a picture of the baby. I watched for it this morning, but they didn't repeat it. Too bad – surely not every baby looked the same!

"Lexie," I said when the grown-ups were gone, "we have to do some work on the horses today. That show is tomorrow. Did you forget?"

She shook her head. "I didn't forget. But I don't know if I can go to the show. I'm too busy watching Mark."

My heart fell. "How long are they staying?" I carried my plate to the sink and rinsed it off. Maria cleaned the table and swept the floor.

"I don't know." She jiggled Mark on her lap and went to her room to find some toys for him. Mrs. Clark had a few, but I guess she figured he needed more. When she returned, she spread a blanket on the grass on the back lawn and settled beside him with her book.

I followed, but I didn't want to read. I wanted to practice.

She shaded her eyes. "Why don't you work out Honey? I'll come down in a little while."

I was more than disappointed. I was angry. It seemed like all she was concerned about was that kid! And I wasn't sure if she was even being paid to watch him. But that didn't seem to matter. The horse show didn't seem to matter to her, either.

I lifted my chin and gritted my teeth. "Okay. I'll do that. If you can't go to the show, I can call a friend of my dad's. He said he'd help out while they were gone. He has a pickup that can pull our trailer. I'm not going to miss the show, Lexie."

She glanced up and raised one eyebrow, like she did to her mom sometimes. "Go ahead."

And that was that.

Brian helped me. He went and got Pepper and the two of us did barrels and practiced dressage. But Honey wouldn't get into her leads properly, and the air was so stifling hot, we were both drenched with sweat before we'd worked very long. I wanted to call it quits. Without Lexie, it just wasn't the same.

Then she appeared, pushing Mark in his stroller, and watched us from the fence. "Slower!" She called. "You're rushing her, Jodi. Keep your reins tight. Sit up straight! Her head *has* to be level with your reins. Yeah, that's better."

When I dismounted and rubbed Honey's head, she came around with Mark. I knew from her face that she was sorry before she even said it.

"Jodi, I'm sorry. I'll go with you to the show, I promise. It's just … sometimes it all overwhelms me and I just want to curl up into a ball and be safe. And with Mark here … well, he's such a doll and I have him for only a little while …" Her voice trailed off and I heard a little quiver in it. She wasn't being a drama queen. I knew she was truly in love with Mark and hated to see him leave.

"That's okay. I know how you feel. I'm sorry, too, for getting mad." I didn't hug her or anything so mushy, but she knew I meant it. "I'll come in with you. Isn't it about time for his nap?"

She nodded and wiped something from her eyes. Brian and I put up the horses and went to the house. Lexie said we could leave Pepper with the other horses – he seemed a little lonely down at our house.

Mrs. Marshal called and said that they were in Quesnel and had decided to get lunch in town. Maria helped us feed Mark and Lexie got him settled for his nap. She stayed in the motor home and I think she took a nap, too. Brian went to play with Roger and Maria had the afternoon off.

And so I found myself alone in the big house. I brought out my new outfit Mom made me for the show and pressed the red satin blouse. Then I watched a bit of Animal Kingdom, tried to get interested in my book, and paced to the living room where I played a piece on the piano.

I was just thinking of taking a walk down to our house to check on the cats when the doorbell rang. I padded to the door, grasped the handle and almost opened it. But something stopped me. I had a horrible thought. *What if someone knows I'm alone…*

I tiptoed to the big bay window and peered out at the front porch. It was a man. I didn't know who he was. He was rather tall and wore a hat. He was dressed in some sort of uniform. I wondered if he was a repairman. But I hadn't heard Mrs. Marshal say anything about a man coming to fix anything.

Should I let him in? What if he's one of the bad guys?

It seemed he stood there for a long time, and every once in a while he'd ring the bell again. *Patient man!* I padded back to the door, but I wasn't about to open it. Then I drew in my breath. The knob turned!

But it was locked. *Whew!* I crept back to the window. *Where's his car?* He jiggled his keys in his pocket, shifted from foot to foot, then finally turned and stepped off the porch. He walked back down the drive. Surely he had a vehicle parked down there somewhere!

I followed him, slipping out of the door as soon as he was beyond earshot. There was a row of thick laurel bushes that lined the drive, so I kept behind them and watched. He went to the main road and climbed into a pickup.

For the second time that day, I gasped. It was an old, yellow pickup, covered with dirt, its front headlight smashed in. *Just like the one Brian had seen in the woods!*

It was hot, but I was suddenly cold, shivers running up and down my arms. He got in the truck and turned it around. I craned my neck to see the license plate number but it was too mucked up with mud to read. About that time, the Marshal's big Explorer pulled into the drive. They looked at me and waved.

I waved back, pretending I was picking something up from the ground.

Lexie got up and brought out Mark. He laughed and reached for Mrs. Clark. She gave him some juice in a bottle. I drew Lexie into her room.

"Something really weird happened just now!"

"Oh, no. Now what?" She grinned when she saw my frown. "Sorry. It just seems like something's always happening around you! What are you – a magnet for trouble?"

I turned away and sat on the bed. "Yeah. Jodi Fischer. The trouble-maker."

"Oh, come on. I didn't say trouble maker. What's going on?" She brushed out her hair and smeared chap stick on her lips. "You're not mad at me again, are you?"

I had to laugh at that. "No. But if you don't listen, I don't know what I'll do." I sniffed and wiped my face. "The doorbell rang and it was a man I didn't know. He was dressed in a uniform, but I didn't think your folks needed a repairman. So I didn't answer the door. I watched him from the window."

As I spoke, she slowly sat down beside me. Her eyes widened and she clenched the bedspread. "Oh wow. What happened then?"

"Well, he left finally. I followed him out to the road. And he got into a battered up old yellow pickup like Brian saw the other day."

"The day the tack room was messed up."

I nodded. "I think we should tell Mr. Walters."

"I'd like to go for a swim."

"That sounds like a good plan." I turned to my suitcase, but stopped when her mom hollered at her from the hall.

"Lexie! Come here, would you, honey?"

Lexie rolled her eyes. "I wonder what she wants me to do now. She never calls me *honey* unless I have to run an errand for her!"

We went to the kitchen where Maria and Traci were having a heated discussion. It turned out that Maria had planned to fix chicken enchiladas that night and Traci bought steaks and wanted Mr. Marshal to grill them. There was further trouble with the menu – Traci also wanted double-baked potatoes and they were out of potatoes.

She turned when we plopped down at the breakfast bar. "I need some baking potatoes, and I found out that Sedge Murray is going to town. I hate to ask you, but do you think you could go in with him and get me some potatoes?"

Lexie sighed elaborately. "Well, we wanted to go swimming, but sure." She eyed me and grinned. "If Jodi can come with me."

"Oh, that's fine. Can you also pick up some ice cream and a cake at the bakery?"

"Vanilla?"

"Any kind you want. Here's the card." She passed over a card and patted Lexie's arm absently. "Thanks, sweetheart. He's leaving in a couple of minutes. Said he'll pick you up out in front."

As we waited outside, I whispered to Lexie, "This is great! We can go see Mr. Walters and tell him what's going on!"

"If we have time."

I lifted my chin. "Well, I'm going there first. You can do your shopping if you want."

"I'm coming with you. Don't think you're going to get rid of me that fast!" We both giggled and about that time, Mr. Murray drove up in his old green Subaru wagon.

If it was hot on the ranch, it was broiling in town. Sedge Murray's car didn't have air conditioning. We kept the windows down, but that didn't help much because he didn't drive over thirty-five the whole way to town. He let us off in front of the Overwaitea store.

But we didn't go there first. Instead, we turned the corner and headed over to the RCMP office. To my relief, Mr. Walters was in his office.

"Come on in, girls," he said with a big grin. "I was just about ready to go home. Got any news?"

I plunked down on a chair and crossed my leg over my knee like I'd seen Mrs. Marshal doing. "Yes! First of all …" I told him about the threatening phone call and about the man who'd come to the door.

He leaned forward. "Do you think you could identify that voice you heard on the phone?"

I shook my head and placed both feet on the floor. "I don't think so. It was a man's. But I was upset, so I didn't think about it much." I twisted a strand of hair between my fingers.

"That's all right." He leaned back and made some notes in a small notebook. "Someone must be watching the house. Did you notice the make of the pickup or the license number?"

"The pickup was an old model, dented in, and it had one headlight smashed out. That's all I can tell you about it. There was mud on the license plate. But the man – I got a pretty good look at him. I think I could recognize him."

He made some more notes. "Good. You've done an excellent job. I may have you look at some make sheets – photographs of criminals – and see if you can spot him. Excuse me for a moment, please."

When he returned a few moments later, he nodded to Lexie. "I'm going to have a talk with your father, Lexie, and let him know what's going on. You may be restricted a bit in your activities, but try to remember it is for your own good. I don't want you riding up into the woods in the direction of the cabin. Okay? I also need to talk to your hired hand. What is his name?"

"Sedge Murray," she said, frowning. "Why do you need to talk to him?"

"Well, he's about to receive a house guest for a little while. I'm assigning one of my best men to cover your place out there. He will pose as Mr. Murray's cousin. His name is Smithers. If you see anything, or hear anything, go right to him. He'll know what to do. Do you have Mr. Murray's phone number?"

"He's in town right now." I stood up. "In fact, he's probably waiting for us. We can show you where he's parked."

Mr. Walters shook his head. "Why don't you tell him what I want to do, and ask him to call me. Here's my phone number." He gave me his card. I must have looked disappointed because he hurried on to explain. "I don't want to endanger you girls any further. I suspect they have men stationed around, watching your movements. Well, keep in touch. I'll see you soon." He escorted us to the door, then hurried down the hall.

Mr. Murray was in his car. Lexie leaned down and spoke with him. "We have to go get some groceries and a cake from the bakery. Shouldn't take too long. I hope you're not too hot."

He shook his head and turned down his radio. He'd had symphony music playing. Probably Mozart. "No. I am fine. But hurry. I need to feed the horses soon."

I followed Lexie's long strides to the store. We were out of breath when we went in.

"The ice cream's down that aisle," she said. "You go get that and I'll get the potatoes. Meet you at the check-out stand."

I headed down the frozen goods aisle and grabbed a half-gallon of vanilla ice cream. Then I turned. And stopped. There, with his back turned to me, was Colton! He was choosing a package of frozen ice cream bars. I whirled and ran back down the other way.

Lexie was coming along the aisle with a bag of potatoes. When she saw me, she said, "What's going on? Why are you so scared?"

"I saw Colton! He was in the frozen section. Let's see if we can spot him again." We crept around the corner. "Hey, look where he's at now! In the *baby food* section!"

We grabbed each other's arms and edged backward, around the corner. I hugged the ice cream to my chest. "We can't let him see us! Look! He's heading to the check-out stand. C'mon!"

"Maybe we can call Mr. Walters and point out Colton to him," Lexie whispered in my ear as we stood in line. She drew out her phone and punched in the number, but he didn't answer.

Colton's line was faster than ours (wouldn't you know!). He paid for his purchases and left the store.

Lexie sighed as she set the bag of potatoes on the moving counter. "Oh, well. It was a good try. Let's get over to the bakery and get a cake. Mom said she'd call."

As we hurried down the sidewalk in the direction of the bakery, I had a strange feeling. I glanced back once, then again. It was as I thought. A man walked along behind us, about half-way down the sidewalk. I was sure he was following us.

CHAPTER EIGHT

Show Time!

We ducked into the bakery and while Lexie made her purchase at the tall counter, I kept watch on the parking lot and sidewalk from the big window. A man loitered at the movie rental store across the street, but he wasn't the one who had been trailing us down the street. No, that man was broad-shouldered, heavy set and wore a cowboy hat. Well, he might have taken off the hat.

Suddenly I saw him again. He was talking to someone who sat in a car at the curb. He straightened and glanced toward the bakery. The hat shadowed his face. I couldn't see his features very well, but I would recognize his build. The way he held himself.

"Okay, let's go. The ice cream is going to be mush." Lexie nudged my elbow.

"That's him, Lexie! Look! The one who was following us!" I pointed to the street, but he was gone. "Oh, shoot. He must've gotten in that car."

Her eyes widened and the grip on my arm intensified. "What are we going to do?"

"Let's get back to Sedge. If we stay around all these people, they won't do anything. Especially not in broad daylight."

I opened the door and we stepped outside. I wanted to scream and run for the safety of the RCMP office but she kept her grip on my arm and we walked calmly to where Sedge was patiently waiting. I glanced around several times, but didn't see the man again.

That evening, during dinner, my dislike for Mr. Clark grew. He seemed to be watching me with cold, black eyes. The more he watched, the more nervous I became, until I spilled my milk. Both Lexie and I jumped at the same time to mop it up.

Brian gave me a lop-sided grin. "I'm glad someone *else* does it."

I wanted to clobber him. A wave of heat flushed up from my neck.

Mr. Clark shook his head. "It's a pity," he said to Mr. Marshal with disgust heavy in his voice, "that you don't have some *decent* neighbors."

Lexie grabbed a wad of paper towels in the kitchen. "Don't let him bother you, Jodi."

But it did. The rest of the meal was hard to endure. Mrs. Clark seemed harsh to Mark and he wailed when she slapped his hand for throwing a cracker on the floor. When he cried, Lexie leaped to her feet and got him out of his chair.

It was nearly dark when I could finally get out of that house and away from those people. I looked over at Sedge Murray's house, but didn't see any strange car parked by his trailer. At the corral, I whistled for Honey, and she came at a trot, her blond mane flowing in the cool evening breeze.

I patted her and fed her an apple, then leaned against her soft, warm body. An owl hooted in the woods and not far away, down by the creek, a cricket band struck up their nightly orchestra. Tears burned my eyeballs. I sniffed and stroked Honey's mane. It felt like a large lump had embedded itself at the back of my throat. Pretty soon, large tears rolled down my cheeks and I let them fall.

"Oh, Honey, I wish I wasn't so afraid all the time and I wish Mom and Dad were back. If only I had someone I could talk to, I mean *really* talk to. I feel so … alone."

Deep in my heart, I heard that same Voice I'd heard before; a whisper, a thought. "I will never leave you, Jodi, or forsake you. You are mine and I love you. Roll your burdens on Me. That's what I'm here for."

I sighed and a small smile found its way to my lips. "Thank You, Lord." Peace flooded my mind. I dug a rumpled hankie from my pocket and blew my nose. Honey tossed her head and walked back over to the other horses. "Tomorrow," I told her just before she left, "we'll show those snooty horses what you can do. Tomorrow we'll win some ribbons, Honey-girl."

She tossed her head once more as if to acknowledge my words, but she was more interested in finding out what Pepper and Cheyenne were doing than in winning ribbons. I cut through the center aisle of the barn and just before I stepped out into the front corral, I heard voices. Men's voices.

I stopped dead.

Somewhere, just outside the barn, two men were talking. I crept forward and peeked around the door. It was Mr. Marshal and Mr. Clark!

They were standing close together, but I could hear their words on the still night air.

Mr. Clark spoke in his gruff voice, "Louise is getting tired of all this monkey business." He lit a cigarette and huffed on it for a bit. "I don't blame her. I am, too. Having to take care of that kid. We're not used to it."

Mr. Marshal coughed. "Well, it won't be much longer. And I promise you, I will pay what we agreed."

"I know that, Dick. How much longer do you think it will ..." He turned and started walking back to the house. I didn't hear the rest of what they said.

But I'd heard enough. What did it mean? Mr. Clark admitted that his wife was not used to taking care of children! Did that mean Mark was not theirs? Whose was he, then? And how did Mr. Marshal fit into this? What kind of a scheme did they have going?

I straightened and moved out into the starlit night. Surely someone as rich as Mr. Marshal wouldn't have to kidnap children to get more money. But I didn't know about his financial situation. I'd bet that Lexie didn't, either. I'd seen Mr. and Mrs. Marshal having fights and from what I could hear of them, it was always about money.

I was confused. Back in Lexie's bedroom, I decided not to tell anyone about what I'd heard. I took a shower and blew my hair dry. Lexie came in and turned on her TV. I joined her on the bed and we watched the news. The one item that we'd been waiting for came at the very end.

"There has been no progress on the Salisbury kidnapping case, police reported today. The deadline for the one million dollars is approaching and the kidnappers have not yet contacted the family as to details on how to deliver the money. It is due by Sunday noon."

I flopped back and groaned. "I hope they catch them. I'm so confused right now; I guess I feel like I can't trust *anyone*. After what I heard your dad saying to Mr. Clark – oops!" I threw my hand over my mouth.

"What did you overhear my dad saying?" Lexie turned down her covers, but the careful way she did it told me she was prickly, ready to defend him.

"I ... uh, mean, about me being clumsy at the dinner table."

Lexie whirled to me and grabbed my shoulders. "C'mon. The truth."

I drew back. "I ... I can't tell you. You'll be ... furious."

"I'm furious right now, Jodi Fischer. So spill it!" She gave me a little shake, then reared back, flopping on the bed. "If you don't, I swear we won't be friends."

I gulped, knowing she didn't mean it. But how could I not tell her? "Oh darn. Well, after dinner tonight I went down to check on Honey, and on the way back, just outside the barn, I saw your dad and Mr. Clark by the corral, talking. I didn't mean to eavesdrop, but ..."

She sat up, her brown eyes huge, her face pale. "Go on." Her voice was very low and calm. The kind of voice she used with Cheyenne when he fought the bit.

I told her what I'd heard.

She sighed and rolled onto her stomach. Then she looked at me with raised eyebrows. "So you think Dad's a crook? That he kidnapped the Salisbury baby and is paying the Clarks to take care of him?"

I shook my head, miserable. I knew it would turn out like this. "I don't know what to think, Lexie! But I suppose … Mr. Walters said not to jump to conclusions. So that means … I don't know. There might be a hundred different meanings to what I overhead them say."

She nodded and flipped her hair back over her shoulder. She straightened her make-up bottles and fingernail paints for quite a while. I leafed through a magazine.

Suddenly she came and sat very close to me, laying a gentle hand on my arm. "I'm sorry I got … upset with you. I can't understand it, either. But I trust my dad and I trust God. That's enough to go on for now."

Tears sprang to my eyes and I hugged her. When we'd wiped our eyes, she smiled at me.

"So are you ready for our big day tomorrow? I have the alarm set for five. Mom has a doctor's appointment but she said she'd be done in time to come and see us ride. Sedge is going to help us load the horses and he'll drive us over to the arena. We have to be there at eight, you know."

"I know." After I brushed my teeth, I climbed into bed. "I don't know if I can sleep, what with thinking about the … mystery, and the horse show. But I hope I can, because I'm going to beat the socks off you tomorrow."

"Dream on."

The alarm rang at five and we bounced out of bed. I brushed my hair, dressed in jeans and a t-shirt and went and shook Brian awake. He'd kill me if I hadn't. Maria made "piggies in a blanket" – sausages wrapped in biscuit dough, baked to a yummy crispness, covered with gravy. My favorite. But my stomach churned so much, I could hardly gulp down one.

One good thing was that the Clarks were gone. I gulped some orange juice and went down to the barn to get the horses ready. I'd come back later for my clothes. We would dress for the show at the arena in the dressing rooms there.

Lexie and Brian came with me. The sun was just topping the ridge above us and I heard a robin and some other bird – I thought it was a finch – in the lilac bushes by the corral. A small breeze nodded the heads of the sunflowers that grew along the fence. It would be a gorgeous day. I couldn't help but feel excited. And happy.

I'd worked with Honey so hard. And now I was going to ride her in a show! Mrs. Marshal said she'd take videos of our ride so Mom and Dad could see my performance. I just wished they could have been here!

Sedge Murray had the trailer backed up to the corral gate, but he was nowhere around. Maybe he'd gone back into the house for breakfast. I still didn't see a strange car there and wondered at that. Maybe Smithers, or whatever his name was, had been dropped off.

We whistled for the horses but they didn't come.

"Those darned horses!" Lexie grumbled. "Wouldn't you know it. The one morning we want them, they have to go up into the woods or down there by the creek. C'mon, you guys. We're going to have to go get them and time is running out."

We grabbed the bridles and stuffed some oats into our jacket pockets to make the actual moment of catching them a little easier. Some horses like to play frisky little games with their owners and lead them on a merry chase around the pasture before being caught. Cheyenne was a little like that and he was teaching Honey. Pepper just followed along with the others. He was a good horse for Brian and the twins, but I was glad Dad had bought me Honey. She was a dream come true.

We covered most of the meadow down by the creek, where the big alder trees grew, and didn't find them. The sun blazed in a deep blue sky, promising a hot day. Already it was too warm for my jacket. I took it off and tied it around my waist.

"Where are they?" Brian puffed behind us, swatting at the no-see-ums, the little tiny bugs that like to bite inside your ear, and paused for a moment beside a fresh pile of manure. "They were here, not long ago."

I nodded. "Let's go look up in the woods. They like to stand up there when the flies get bad."

"We have to *hurry*! We're supposed to be there in …" Lexie glanced at her watch, "about an hour."

"Take it easy," I reminded her, "rushing around and getting a heat stroke isn't going to make it better." I turned to Brian. "Why don't you go get Sedge and see if he can help? Then go up to the house and load our clothes and boots and hats into the pickup. Grab some water, too, okay? I put the cooler out by the back steps."

He nodded and started back to the house. "Okay. Your servant boy hears and obeys."

We didn't wait for Sedge to come. We *couldn't* wait. Now we were possessed with a sort of fever. It twisted my stomach as we called and called – and still no answering whinny or thud of heavy feet on the soft ground. We saw their prints and followed them through the brush.

Why would they just stand in the woods when they could hear us calling? Where were they? It was about then that an awful thought struck me: *what if they'd been stolen? Shot?*

Suddenly I was cold, then hot. I froze for a second, then hurried to catch up with Lexie. In a panic of anxiety and fear, I thrashed about in the woods, still calling. We split up. I could hear her whistle and call. Both of our throats were getting dry.

Where was Sedge? Why hadn't he come?

It was getting late. When I rejoined Lexie, she was sitting on a log, her hair frazzled around her face, tears on her cheeks, fear in her large eyes. "I found where they got through the fence." She took me to a place where the barbed wire was broken, lying on the ground.

"It's been cut," she said with a shaky voice.

I stared at the wire like it would bite me. Then I searched the ground. Sure enough, I saw hoof prints leading out of the pasture, into the woods. "We have to follow them! Hurry! We're going to be late for the show!" I barged ahead, but she pulled me back.

"Let's face it, Jodi. We won't be going to the show." She pushed back her long bangs that had fallen in her face and wiped her eyes.

"But … but we can't be far behind them. We can still make it. We don't ride until ten."

"What if they're …" she couldn't get the word out. It hung in the silence between us. *Dead.* I knew that was what she was going to say.

I started shouting. "They're not! They're not dead! So quit standing around like a dummy and help me find them!"

"Jodi, it doesn't help to holler." She shook me, as if to bring me to my senses. "But I'll come with you. I just want you to know … to prepare yourself that this might not be … good." Big tears rolled down her cheeks.

I wrapped my arms around her and we stood there, sobbing our hearts out on each other's shoulders. Then we pulled apart and blew our noses.

"Okay." I drew a shaky breath. "Let's go. Follow the tracks. We can't be far behind them."

It was not too hard to follow the tracks of three horses. We went through the woods and then out onto the dirt road. Even there, we had no difficulty tracking them. The sun climbed the heavens and sweat soaked my shirt. A crow cawed off in the woods irritatingly and squirrels scolded us from time to time. Those were the only sounds we heard.

I glanced at my watch – especially as it drew near to nine o'clock. I could envision the crowds at the arena, the other contestants and their horses, the excitement and anticipation in the air, the announcer calling out the first class, the smell of hot dogs on the grill. I thought of my new outfit, and I had to stifle my sobs and keep plodding on down the road.

At least we hadn't heard any shots. At least the horses were still alive. *Or were they?*

We were going in the direction of the cabin. Had the horses been driven? A fresh set of car tracks erased most of them in the road – a vehicle had come after the horses. So they *had* been driven!

"Looks like we're heading to the cabin," Lexie said, pausing to wipe her forehead. "Just the place where Mr. Walters said to stay away from. We should've gone back and checked to see if that Smithers guy was at Sedge's place."

"We didn't have time." I motioned to keep going, even though my legs were tired and all I wanted was to find Honey, get on her back, and ride home. "C'mon. We're getting close. This last bit, let's cut through the trees and sneak up on the side of the cabin. We don't want to exactly announce ourselves."

"Wish I had a gun," Lexie muttered.

I laughed despite the fear that tightened my jaw and sent my heart racing. "So you could shoot your foot off?"

She glanced at me and kept walking.

When we could see the cabin roof, I stopped in my tracks and caught my breath. *Oh, dear Lord, please help us find the horses! And help them to be alive!*

"What do we do now?" I could hear Lexie's labored breathing beside me.

We knelt in the fringe of the woods, behind some bushes, and tried to see. There was a pickup parked in front. Smoke came from the chimney. I led the way closer, keeping to the scant cover of the bushes. It crackled under my hands and knees and I stopped frequently, hoping the gang wasn't listening to the noise outside their windows.

Goosebumps rose on my arms, but I ignored them. I was so intent on spotting the horses, I almost crawled right out into the clearing beside the cabin. But I stopped in time and Lexie bumped into me.

"*What?* What do you see?" she hissed.

I craned my neck and sure enough, I saw Cheyenne's legs and his bright red coat, just a flash of it, and then – *yes!* – I saw Honey's creamy tail swishing and Pepper's white head. "The horses are there! They're right in front of the cabin!"

"Oh, no!" She groaned. "How are we going to get them?"

I didn't answer because right then someone came out. I scrunched down and pulled Lexie with me, but I could still see through an opening in the bush. It was a man – I could swear it was the same man who'd followed us yesterday in Quesnel!

I gasped, and would've stood up, but Lexie was holding onto my arm.

"What?"

"He has a gun!" I threw my hand over my mouth.

The man's voice floated over to me clearly. "What's goin' on?"

"Boss! Stop! We can take them back – say it was just a mistake, or …"

"No, I tell you! There's only one thing we can do!" He raised the rifle to his shoulder.

I don't know if I screamed or not, but suddenly ... *boom!* the gun blasted.

The sound seemed to pierce my heart. My eyes were closed but tears escaped them and rolled down my cheeks. Honey was gone. I just knew it.

CHAPTER NINE

A Surprise

"No, no, no!" At first I didn't know who was talking, then I realized it was my own voice, moaning deep in my throat. I opened my eyes and peeked through my fingers. Had they shot the horses? Which one would I see lying on the ground, bleeding? Would there be two more shots? But there was only dust in the clearing – no horses, no men. I caught the swish of a tail around the far corner.

"They just scared them!" Lexie scrambled to her feet and yanked on my arm. She led the way back into the woods, pulling me along with her. "C'mon, Jodi, we gotta get them!"

We tore through those woods like frightened deer, only not so agile. I ripped my jeans and scraped my knee on a branch; Lexie tripped and fell over a fallen log. It seemed to take forever, but finally we were out on the road and the horses were just in front of us.

They snorted and tossed their heads, but we were far enough from the cabin that we could call their names. They showed the whites of their eyes, but they recognized us and slowed to a walk.

I dug in my pocket and found a few grains of oats. "C'mon, Honey-girl. Here, Pepper. C'mon, boy. That's a good boy." Pepper allowed me to approach.

Lexie had a time with Cheyenne, because he's more high strung than either of ours, but finally she got the bridle on him. I strapped the bridle on Honey. I didn't bother with Pepper. He'd come along behind us.

Lexie had to lead Cheyenne to a stump to get on, but I jumped up on Honey from the ground. Soon we were trotting briskly down the road.

"Man, it sure feels good to be riding again." I ran my hand through my hair. "I thought for sure he was going to shoot them. Didn't you?"

She nodded, her lips still rimmed with white, her eyes huge. "Yeah. But those men would have had plenty of trouble if they'd shot Cheyenne! My dad would've skinned them alive."

I laughed, trying to picture Mr. Always Correct and Perfect skinning a person! Then another thought hit me – *unless he's in with them! Maybe that's why they didn't shoot them!* But I pushed the thought away. It was way too mean, and here I was, jumping to conclusions again.

"I think they were just trying to scare us," she said in a low voice.

"Well, they did a pretty good job of it. Do you think they knew we were watching?"

She shook her head. "No. But they knew we'd miss them by now. And come looking. And that we'd miss the show." She paused and shot me a glance. "I'm sorry about that, Jodi. I know you were looking forward to it."

"That's okay. There'll be more shows. Maybe God knew that Honey and I weren't quite ready." I thought about all that had happened and the shock of it made me tremble. Even when it was over. I'd heard of people who were more scared after the thing happened than during it.

Well, when we arrived at the corral and I slid off Honey, my knees gave out on me and I almost landed on the ground. I caught myself in time. Brian came bursting from the house and Sedge Murray appeared from the barn.

We explained to both of them what had happened. Without a word, Sedge got his tools and started up into the woods to mend the fence. After he left, a small, dark man came into the corral. He was maybe in his early thirties, had light hair and a nice smile. He wore jeans, a t-shirt and a baseball cap that had *Seattle Mariners* on it. He stepped across the open corral, avoiding the piles of manure, and approached us with a smile.

He held out his hand to Lexie. "Hello. I'm Mr. Smithers, Sedge Murray's cousin. I heard the commotion and I wanted to know if I could help. You had trouble with the horses?"

Lexie tucked a strand of dark hair behind her ear. "Yeah. They got loose."

"Actually, the wire was cut," I said, stepping forward. "And the horses were herded up to the cabin by a pickup." I told him the rest, and at the end I said, "Oh. Sorry. My name's Jodi Fischer, Lexie's friend."

He shook my hand soberly. There was a glint in his blue eyes, as if he was thinking a lot more than he was saying. "Nice to meet you, Jodi. I've heard a lot about you." He removed his baseball cap, smoothed down his blond hair, and returned the cap to his head.

"Well, let's see what we have here. Would you come over to the trailer and give me a full report? It won't take long."

"Lexie, you gotta call your mom," Brian said as we followed Mr. Smithers to the trailer. He handed Jodi his phone. "She's been calling the house phone and I didn't have anything to tell her, except that the horses were missing. And that you'd gone to find them."

She punched in the number and in a few minutes she was talking to her mom. I heard her relate a shortened account of the events, then, "Uh, huh. Uh, huh. Yes, Mother. Bye."

"She okay?" I asked as we entered Sedge Murray's small trailer. It was very neat. Mr. Smithers led us to the pocket-sized living room.

Lexie shrugged. "A little worried, but she's all right. Says she'll be home soon."

We sat down. Mr. Smithers leaned forward on the chair, a smile on his face. "You know who I am and what I'm doing here. So we can skip right to the important matters." He drew out a laptop and poised his fingers above the keyboard. "What was going on this morning? Jodi, you begin, and the others keep quiet, please. You will each have a turn to tell your version of it."

I told him everything that had happened, even being followed in town yesterday, and the description of the man who had followed us.

"What was the vehicle like where he spoke to that man?"

"It was a black SUV – I think an Explorer, or something like that. The pickup we saw at the cabin wasn't the old yellow one Brian saw in the woods. The one today was red. Right, Lexie?"

She nodded. "Yeah. I think it was a Ford Ram, but I'm not sure."

He nodded, typing away furiously as we spoke. "Go on."

I told him about the men at the cabin and how they shot off the rifle. "Must have been over the heads of the horses. They were scared, but unharmed."

"Okay. Now, you, Lexie. Tell me your version." He mostly listened as she talked and made a few more notes. After she was finished, Brian told him what had happened at the house, which wasn't much. Sedge, it turned out, had received a phone call about the time we went looking for the horses, and since he didn't have a cell phone, had to talk in his trailer.

"And Colton," I murmured. "He just keeps popping up everywhere."

Mr. Smithers raised his eyebrows. "Colton? Do you have a last name?"

"Somonivich, something like that. He's ... he's in grade twelve, but he's older, he must have been kept back in school. I'd say he's around twenty."

"What else do you know about him?"

I shrugged. "Not much. He's a foster child. I don't know where he lives. Mostly on the street, I think. He always hangs around the worst guys in school. I've heard rumors he does drugs, but I can't say for sure."

He typed away, stopped and looked up. "Okay. We'll check out these leads. I'm going to stake out the cabin tomorrow. Please stay fairly close to the house and barn, okay?"

"Mr. Smithers, what's going on? What do you suspect?"

He shook his head, his eyes steely gray now. "Too early to tell. Drugs, almost certainly. What else – I don't know. These guys play for keeps, though. We don't want anyone getting hurt, so do as I say, okay?" He looked at Lexie. "I'd like to borrow a horse. Do you have one that's not too high strung? I haven't ridden for awhile, but I think it would be the best way to get up there and do some surveillance."

Lexie nodded. "Sure. Lady is real tame. I'll get her ready for you. When do you want to go?"

"As soon as possible."

We went up to the house. Mrs. Marshal returned home and we told her what happened. While she got lunch ready, we saddled Lady and got Mr. Smithers off on his ride.

Lunch was a sorry affair since Maria had the day off and Lexie's mom isn't that great of a cook. In spite of the trouble with the horses, Traci seemed excited and sort of weird, like she was excited about something and was keeping it a secret.

But none of us shared her happy mood. Silence fell on the dining room like a dark cloak. Clouds covered the bright, sunny day and it felt like rain.

Traci dabbed her mouth with a napkin and pushed back her chair. We helped her clean up the kitchen. "Kids, you're just too gloomy for words. Let's do something fun. How about a movie? I'll take you in and come and get you after."

I was more than surprised. We checked the theater offerings online and found a cartoon we'd been wanting to see forever. I changed clothes and got my purse, then joined the others in the foyer. Brian had even combed his hair and put on a clean shirt. I couldn't believe it.

Traci bought us the tickets, a huge bin of popcorn, and large enough cups of pop to drown in. We got settled in the theater, and were chatting happily, when someone came and plunked themselves down beside me. I moved my purse to the other side, next to Brian, and glanced their way.

My heart fell. It was Colton!

He didn't say much throughout the movie. I didn't want to sit beside him, but I kept thinking what Mom would say, "Be nice to him. Maybe you can help him understand about God's love." We even passed the popcorn down to him. But I wouldn't share my pop. Not with him!

At the end, we stood and gathered our things. The others filed down the row. I felt Colton tug on my shirt.

"Hey, I heard you had a little fun this morning with your horses."

I turned and stared at him, jolted out of my good mood. "I wouldn't call it fun, buster," I said through gritted teeth. "Scaring our horses isn't very nice. Scaring us is even worse. What's your game, Colton? Why don't you pick on someone your own size?"

He winced at that. I saw that I'd struck a nerve. But then a sneer twisted his mouth. "That's your view of it. You've been warned and you haven't listened. So listen now. You keep to your side of the woods and leave us alone. You hear?" He shoved his dirty face next to mine.

I recoiled at the smell of alcohol on his breath. "Or what?"

"You'll find out. Houses burn, you know. So watch out and keep your nose outta our business." He turned and walked down the aisle the opposite way.

I ran to catch up with the others, my mind awhirl, my heart thudding heavily. "Oh, man, Lexie, wait!" I pulled her back. We went in the girl's bathroom and I told her in a whisper while we washed our hands.

She shook her head. "Just stay away from him, Jodi."

"I *can't!*" I looked at her as she brushed her hair. "What's the matter with you? I thought ... we were together in this."

She sighed heavily and turned to face me, like she always did when she was upset. "We are. But I don't ... I can't ...I don't know, it's just too big for us. We have to back out and let the RCMP do it. It's their job."

"Uh, huh. And how much have they done so far?" I grabbed her arm. "Please, Lexie. For once listen to me. I can't ..."

She shoved my hands away, turned abruptly and ran out the door.

I followed, fighting tears. If I didn't have Lexie's support, I might as well give up.

But how could I? They'd threatened the horses, a baby's life was at stake, and now they hinted they might burn down our house! I didn't doubt for a second that they could – and would. And all I really wanted was to be safe. To get rid of the fear that haunted my dreams and stalked my waking hours like a vampire. But it seemed the events of the last few days had mired me more and more into fear.

Mrs. Marshal took us over to the arena where there were some afternoon shows. We watched the contestants for awhile, but I knew Brian was bored and I was getting restless. Traci took us next to the Dairy Queen and bought us ice cream cones. After that, we headed home.

Lexie was quiet all the way back. I wrote her a note. "Let's go swimming when we get home."

She grinned when she read it. "Sounds good to me," she wrote back. Then she took the paper from me and wrote, "Mom said she and Dad have a surprise for me tonight. I wonder what it is."

I drew a smiley face on the bottom, then a big question mark. It was something at least to take our minds off the horses and everything else that was happening. Lexie wasn't the only one who was scared out of her socks and wanted to escape. I did, too. It felt like a huge steam train was bearing down on me and I had nowhere to go.

Maria was back in time for dinner. Her fish tacos were absolutely delicious, and her strawberry shortcake topped off the meal just perfectly. Yum! Lexie went to the living room with her folks, while Brian and I sat on the swing in the back yard.

I called Mom. She'd told me to call her every night around eight. I'd missed one or two nights, but most times I remembered. My reports of our day's events had included nothing of the mystery that had so engulfed us all. But this night I told her the horses got out and when Mom kept asking questions, I finally broke down and told her what was going on.

She was upset, but I assured her we were okay and that the police had stationed a man here to watch the place -- or they *had*. I didn't mention he was gone. When she'd calmed down, she said, "We love you, sweetie. Keep your chin up. We'll be home on Sunday. Now put Brian on, okay?"

"Okay, Mom. Love you, too. Tell Dad hi." I wiped my eyes and handed the phone to Brian.

We swam in the cool of the evening, and after that, Brian and I watched TV in Lexie's room. When she joined us, she was absolutely beaming. I'd never seen her so happy.

"What's going on?" I fluffed up the pillow and twiddled with a strand of my hair.

"Oh, Jodi!" She gushed, grabbing up her stuffed lion. She doesn't usually gush, so she got my attention. "Mother and Dad told me they're going to *adopt a baby*!"

"Wow." It took my breath away. "Is it … anyone we know?"

She laughed. "Of course not. They're just investigating it, and said it might take a long time, that I shouldn't get my hopes up too much. But isn't it just *awesome*?"

"Cool," Brian said. I could tell he was out of his depth, but he remembered his manners. "That's great, Lexie." Big yawn. "Guess I'll turn in."

We hugged each other joyfully when he left. Lexie wiped her eyes and blew her nose with a tissue. "This is the biggest thing that's ever happened! I just can't believe it. We could never convince Mom before to do it before." She pulled out her diary to make an entry. "But I feel so bad about the Salisbury baby. Did you hear the news? Have they found out anything yet?"

I shook my head slowly, sad to give her bad news. Brian and I heard a short story on it, but it was not good. "They said that the deadline's still set for Sunday. Tomorrow! Lexie, if that baby dies, I'm going to die, too."

All her joy seemed to drain away. She flung herself on the bed and nodded solemnly. "I'm sorry I … like, flaked out on you earlier. I want to solve this mystery if it helps that little boy." She shivered. "I sure hope something happens, so we can get done with this. Like soon."

"It will," I said, grasping a large stuffed bear to my chest, "I can feel it in the air."

CHAPTER TEN

Back to the Cabin!

The wind died and the stars were out. We went out and jumped on the trampoline for awhile, then laid down on it and watched for falling stars. I kept looking into the dark woods that ringed the pasture, wondering who was out there, watching us. What had Mr. Smithers found out at the cabin? I was sure he knew more than he was saying. Was it really the kidnappers? Had they gotten him, too?

Lexie glanced over at me and raised herself up on one elbow. "Lady's not in the corral. I wonder what's taking Mr. Smithers so long."

"That's what I was wondering myself. You know, he said we couldn't go up to the cabin, but maybe we could ride part ways and see if he's coming home. He might like the company."

Lexie hugged her knees to her chest. "I don't know if we should. The woods are scary at night – even without a gang of criminals hanging out in them."

I rubbed the shivers off my arms, trying to calm the panic that was always in the back of my mind. "But if I don't *do* something, I'm going to go crazy! I would sure like to find that other sock and the missing half of that note." I paused, listening to the crickets.

"Oh, c'mon! It won't hurt to go just a little ways!"

We bridled the horses and jumped on bareback. I opened the gate and closed it after Lexie rode through. "Let's go along that path through the woods. Isn't that the way you told Mr. Smithers to go?"

"I drew him a map. I hope he's not lost."

We rode up through the woods, found another gate, and continued on, past the road. I knew this path connected to the road further up, closer to the cabin. After awhile, I drew rein and glanced back as Lexie rode up on Cheyenne. "I wonder where we are now."

She looked around, even though you couldn't see much. "I don't know, but we've come far enough. It's too dark and we must be pretty close to the cabin."

"No, we haven't come that far. Do you think – Sh!" I listened, hard. "Did you hear that? It's like someone – "

"Sh!"

There! It came again. The crackling noise of someone coming through the brush.

"Maybe it's Mr. Smithers on Lady," she whispered in my ear.

"Let's get the horses off the trail in case it isn't him." We dismounted and led them off the track, tying them to slender alder trees. We crept back. Hiding behind a screen of bushes, we watched the trail. Suddenly Lexie gripped my arm. I almost screamed. There, coming down the trail, was a man!

I bit my nails. I wanted to run, but my legs felt like butter that's been left out in the sun too long. I kept telling myself it was Mr. Smithers. It had to be Mr. Smithers! But it wasn't.

As he drew closer, I saw in the dim starlight that he had wide shoulders, was tall, and wore a beard. He was carrying several bags. I held my breath, afraid to move, until he disappeared down the trail. Then I realized I had a death grip on Lexie's hand.

"That's not our detective friend," Lexie whispered. "I wonder who it was. He looked familiar somehow."

I let out the breath I'd been holding. "I don't know. It's too dark to see. Let's get out of here and find Mr. Smithers."

We untied the horses. I helped her mount, then jumped up on Honey.

"Which way do we go?" Lexie held Cheyenne back. He wanted to return to his stall in the worst way.

"Let's go on the road. It's the fastest, and I don't think it's very far away. Just through those trees. C'mon."

She was right -- we hit the road in a few minutes and then kicked our horses and headed for home. It was a relief to come out in the pasture after being in the dark woods. We rode up to the barn and swung down. It was then that I noticed Lady, munching grass a little ways away.

"Mr. Smithers is back," Lexie said as we carried the bridles to the tack room. "Let's go over and see him."

When Sedge Murray opened the door of the trailer, I stepped up on the first step. "Is Mr. Smithers here?"

He shook his head. "No. He came back from his ride a little while ago. Then he packed his things and left. He said something about a ... I don't know ... a break through. Whatever *that* means." He paused and almost shut the door. After a bit, he returned, grasping a white envelope. "Oh, wait! There *is* something else. He wrote you this and said to give it to you. And … and after you read it, he said to burn it." He shook his head and turned away.

I took the envelope and thanked him, but my mind was whirling and disappointment crashed upon me like a ten-ton weight. Just when we needed him, he had to leave!

In Lexie's room, we opened the letter. I read it out loud while she peered anxiously over my shoulder.

"Girls, I'm in a hurry, so this will be short. I spent most of the day watching the cabin. I took some pictures and videos. Most of what I discovered, I can't tell you. Mr. Walters called me away as there is a breakthrough on the kidnapping case. Please stay close to home tomorrow. Mr. Smithers."

"Wow!" I used the letter to van my face. "I wonder if he's connecting the mystery at the cabin with the kidnapping!" I read the note again.

Lexie went to her dressing table and began filing her nails. "But why would he leave, if that were the case? Why wouldn't they surround the cabin with police and rescue the baby?"

I scratched my head. "There's something more to it that he can't tell us about. He did mention drugs. I wonder if he's suspecting drugs up there."

Lexie threw down her file and paced to the window. "I'm not so sure I want to go to sleep, knowing that our detective is gone. And that threat about your house – what if they – "

"Stop!" I stuffed a pillow around my head. When I emerged, I sighed. "We just have to trust God, Lexie. That's all we can do."

She agreed and we prayed about it. My private prayer was, "Lord, please send someone I can talk to about this, because I'm really scared and I don't know what to do."

Big, black thunder clouds perched on the horizon and the humidity off the radar the next morning. I rolled out of bed and got a shower. Lexie was already up, had made her bed, and was off somewhere. *This is the day! Tomorrow's the last day of the deadline for the Salisburys!* A sense of dread rolled over me. I dressed in shorts and a t-shirt and ran a comb through my curly hair.

Maria made Brian and I some scrambled eggs and toast for breakfast. We ate together at the small kitchen table, and after that, he went down to our house to feed the cats and check on the cows. As the morning dragged by, I remembered what Lexie said she had to do – a doctor's appointment. Lucky girl! I wandered to the barn and saddled Honey.

I took her through her steps and did the barrels a couple of times, but my heart wasn't in it, and hers wasn't, either. "Well, Honey-girl, let's call it a day." I released her with a pat and returned the bridle and saddle to the tack room. Just as I slipped the bridle over the nail, a board squeaked loudly in another part of the barn. I stood still, listening. Was Sedge cleaning?

I stepped out into the wide hallway. No one was around. Was it just my imagination? I swept my hair back and swallowed hard, fighting down the fear the crept up my back. No, I was sure I'd heard something.

I started back to the house, but saw a red car parked in the driveway. A young man, dressed in nice slacks and a polo shirt, was walking around the back of the house, saw me, and came on down to the barn. It was Dave Reilly, the youth leader at our church. My heart jumped. Just the person I could maybe talk to! But was he in too much of a hurry.

"Hi, Jodi," he said with a big grin. "I went to your house and Brian said you were here. I was wondering if you'd play your guitar for our youth meeting next week. And sing."

I felt my face flush and lowered my eyes. "I'm not that good. Lexie's the singer, you know."

"Fine." He nodded as if it was all decided. "You can do a duet, then. But I've heard you play, Jodi, and you're good, whether you want to admit it or not. I'll figure on you doing something, then."

It was hard, if not impossible, to refuse him. "Well, okay. I … um, I was wondering if I could ask you a question?"

His hazel eyes softened and he faced me. "Sure." We walked to the corral where hooked his foot on the lower rail, and looked at the horses. "Is that your bay over there? The thoroughbred?"

I saw he knew something about horses, which is cool. "No, that's Lexie's horse, Cheyenne. Mine's over there. The palomino quarter horse. She just rolled in the dirt. I had her all brushed off a couple of minutes ago."

"She's nice, even though a little dirty." We laughed. He leaned on the fence. "Now what did you want to ask me?"

I kicked the dirt, unsure of how to begin. "It's kind of hard to put into words, but I was wondering how … how do you know what God wants you to do?"

"Well, He's given us a Guidebook, you know." He rubbed his chin and I saw the wedding ring on his finger glint in a ray of sunshine that escaped the clouds. He'd been married only six months. I'd helped serve for their reception. "The Bible gives us a lot of wisdom if we dig it out. Take the book of Proverbs. It's full of all kinds of advice on how to live in a wise, godly way. Can you tell me your particular problem?"

We watched as Sedge emerged from his trailer and went to the barn.

"Well, not exactly. But it's about someone who needs help and it's ... well, it may be dangerous. Maybe it's not my business, but somehow I feel it is. I feel like I should do something about it."

He smiled. "That doesn't tell me much. But I know this much: sometimes we get into a lot of trouble by barging into places we should've stayed away from." He snatched a weed and broke it into small pieces. "And sometimes we don't do enough."

"How can we know the difference?"

"I guess that takes wisdom. And being in tune with the Spirit of God. We should be walking close to God and reading His Word, and when we're faced with a decision, we can hear His voice speaking to us. And we'll know what to do."

I grimaced. "That sounds easy. But it gets mixed up in real life."

"I know." He laughed. "I'd like you to work on something for me. First of all, commit this problem to the Lord and ask Him to show you what He wants you to do. If it's something sinful, you know you can't do it." He pierced me with a bright glance.

I shook my head. "Oh, no. It's not like that."

"Okay. I want you to sit down and read through the book of Proverbs. As you do, write down all the verses that might give you clues as to what God wants you to do."

I stared at him. "The whole book?"

"Well, as much as you can. That should keep you busy for awhile."

"No kidding." I looked up at him and smiled. "Thanks for listening, Dave."

"No problem. I'll be praying for you." He gave me a little wave and strode to his car.

I was a little disappointed that he hadn't told me what I should do, but I sighed and went back to the house. Brian was back, and so was Lexie and her mom.

"Hey, guess what!" Lexie met me in the foyer. She'd changed already into shorts and a tank top, with a green baseball cap topping her dark hair. She looked cute.

"What?"

"Mom said she'd take us to a ball game this afternoon. And you know who's playing?"

I didn't have to guess. The way her brown eyes twinkled, I knew. "Bob Carson," I said, putting my shoes in the closet.

"Yeah!" She led the way to the family room and plopped down on the sofa. "You coming?"

I shook my head. "No, I want to do some reading. I'm kind of tired. Hope I'm not getting sick."

We ate lunch out on the deck and laughed at the birds at the feeder. Before she left, I asked her to get the words we'd copied from the note in the sock. She looked at me strangely, but fetched it, and with a water bottle and her camera, she and Brian left with her mom.

Maria was making something in the kitchen and the big grandfather clock in the living room ticked-tocked loudly. I settled down at Mr. Marshal's desk in the study with my Bible and a notebook. I hadn't read far when the words seemed to leap at me from the page with the force of a sudden blow.

Quickly I wrote them down, "Then you will walk in your way securely and your foot will not stumble. When you get up, you will not be afraid; when you lie down, your sleep will be sweet. Do not be afraid of sudden fear nor of the onslaught of the wicked when it comes, for the Lord will be your confidence and will keep your foot from being caught. Do not withhold good from those to whom it is due, when it is in your power to do it." Proverbs 3:23-27

I paused and read what I'd just written down. Then I studied the note from the sock. It struck me that I'd never done anything to help the situation. But now! Now it was the afternoon of the last day that the kidnappers had given for a deadline. Should I return to the cabin and investigate it?

I rubbed my forehead where a headache was forming. My stomach didn't feel good, either. A storm was brewing again – I could feel it. I turned back to the Bible and leafed through some more of Proverbs. There was lots of advice there, but my mind kept going back to the words, "Do not withhold good... Do not withhold good... "

Finally I laid down my pen and closed my eyes. "Lord, show me what I should do. Maybe I can't help at all. But I only know one thing that might save that baby's life, And that's to find the other half of this note. Help me not to be afraid!" I drew a breath and exhaled it slowly, fighting against tears. "Thank You, Lord."

I wrote a short note to Lexie and left it on her bed. After that, I went down to the barn, caught Honey, groomed her, put the saddle on, and started up into the woods in the direction of the cabin. I hoped the storm wouldn't break before I got back. Black clouds piled on top of one another, blocking out the sun, and promising rain.

The woods were still, almost as if all the forest creatures were holding their breaths, waiting for the storm. I couldn't help but look over my shoulder every once in a while, as if someone were watching me. Maybe they were!

As I approached the cabin, my uneasiness grew. I pulled back on the reins where the log had once blocked the road. A rumble of thunder rolled across the hills. What should I do now?

I turned Honey into the woods and rode up behind the cabin. Peering through the trees, I saw there weren't any cars or trucks parked around it. Dismounting, I tied Honey to a bush, patting her neck. "We're in for it, girl." I crept to the row of bushes where I could watch the cabin.

The rain started with a gentle *pitter-pat* on the leaves of the bushes and quickly grew to a heavy downpour. Honey shifted restlessly when the thunder came closer and lightning lit the darkening sky. I hugged my knees to my chest and was glad I'd worn my jacket.

Suddenly I realized there was no smoke coming from the chimney! No smoke, no cars, no signs of life. Was it empty? Had those people left?

Rain was falling steadily when I stepped out from behind the bushes and crept closer to the cabin, keeping on the side that didn't have any windows. I listened for voices, for footfalls on a wooden floor. Nothing.

Slowly I worked my way around to the front. Silence greeted me. A crow cawed from the top of a pine nearby. How could I find out if they were gone or merely sleeping? I looked around. Ah! A stone. I picked it up and chucked it onto the planks that formed the porch. It rattled across and lay still.

Nothing. I threw another one, this time a larger rock. Still nothing. Gaining confidence, I mounted the steps, tiptoed across the porch and slowly opened the door.

CHAPTER ELEVEN

A Light in the Window

The one-room log cabin was empty.

I stepped through the door and looked around. It was a mess! Someone had been here and left in such a hurry that they hadn't bothered to pick anything up. Garbage, bed clothes, tin cans, paper, stray socks and a lot of other things lay strewn across the wooden planks. In one corner, an old table stood. It was covered with paper plates, cold food and beer cans. In another corner stood an old wood stove made of tin. Beds covered one wall, with sleeping bags in a heap on them.

I propped open the door with a stick of firewood, wishing I could start the fire. I shivered It was cold in the cabin. Signs that a baby had been there were everywhere. Empty tin cans of formula, dirty disposable diapers, and even a filthy, ragged blanket lay amid the junk of the floor. But was that proof that this baby was the kidnapped Salisbury child? I rested my hands on my hips, disgusted. "How am I ever going to find anything in a mess like this?"

The old cabin timbers creaked with the storm. I could hear the scurry of mice. I shivered again and zipped up my jacket. *What if those people come back suddenly and creep up on me?* I glanced out the plastic-covered window. *I'd better hurry and find that sock, if it's here!*

Beginning to the left of the door, I started searching through the trash. It wasn't a very pleasant job. I looked through bags of garbage, under the beds, under the mattresses; I picked up and shook out all the blankets and sleeping bags, and finally I'd made it all the way around the cabin.

I plunked down on one of the wobbly wooden chairs and sighed. My stomach was bothering me again. Looking through all that garbage hadn't helped it any! It was getting dark. Where could that sock be? Had they taken it? Was it ever here in the first place?

Suddenly I saw something I'd hadn't noticed before. It was a wood box behind the stove. I sighed and stood up. I must have been wrong – the sock wasn't here. Maybe the people who were here weren't the kidnappers, after all.

I strolled to the wood box and lifted the lid. And gasped. So here was where they hid the baby! Inside was a car seat. When someone came, this would have been an excellent place to hide him! Eagerly I pulled out the blankets and shook them out.

Something fell to the floor. *A blue sock!* I snatched it up and smoothed it out on my hand. Was there a note in this one, too? I felt it and pulled the yarn apart. No. My heart fell. Nothing in this one, then.

A ray of sunshine, escaping from behind the clouds that were parting, found its way into the window and lit on the box. Almost like the finger of God, pointing the way. I looked again inside the box. Lifted out the bed. Rummaged around in the wood chips. The light faded. It was hard to see.

I picked up a larger piece of wood on the bottom of the box and squealed. In the corner, I saw a wadded up piece of paper. With trembling fingers, I brought it out to the porch where the light was better. When I'd smoothed it out, I saw the words.

Quickly I brought out the paper from home. The words matched! I read out loud, "We will ask one million in cash for the baby's safe return. We will find a place near Quesnel to hide the baby. Contact Colton S. for a place. He will be your errand boy. Promise him anything."

Wow! *So it was true! The kidnappers were really here and they had the baby!* I tried to keep calm, but it was hard to focus on anything but the danger I'd put myself in. My hand shook like a leaf in the wind, and my knees were wobbly, like newborn foals when they take their first steps. Then another thought struck me – *where are they now?*

I sent a frantic plea to heaven for help and stuffed the notes into my pocket. I ran to Honey, untied her, and got in the saddle. The rain turned to a drizzle. It was a long, wet ride home under the dripping trees. Honey was as anxious as I was to get home, so we made it in record time.

As we reached the pasture and I piled off to open the gate, I realized how late it had gotten. Maybe it was just darker than usual because of the storm. Anyhow, when I got back into the saddle, I glanced at the barn. Suddenly I saw a flash of light from one of the upper windows. In the hay loft.

What was that? Surely Sedge wouldn't be up there. I dismounted by the corral and glanced over at his trailer. His car was gone. No, it wouldn't be him. I heard a vehicle out on the road, passing by. *Oh. It must have been a reflection of car lights from the road.*

But a funny, tingly feeling remained as I unsaddled Honey and took the bridle off her head. I whistled a tune and stepped up to the big double doorway of the barn.

Just as I was going to place my foot on the doorsill, I stopped. My foot was midair, halfway to the board, dangling there like it didn't know where to go. Something stopped it from resting on the floor of the barn! Slowly I brought it back and stood still. Quietly I waited there in the dark, wondering what I should do.

The shivery feeling came back, ten times as bad. I found myself listening, holding my breath. What had stopped me from walking into the barn? Something strange was going on, but what? I didn't know.

Finally I hung the bridle on the corral fence post and ran up to the house. When I was in the back yard, I looked back at the barn. It stood dark and silent, almost ominous, like it was guarding a strange secret.

CHAPTER TWELVE

A Journey in the Dark

"Hey! Where've you been?" Brian greeted me as I stepped into the kitchen from the deck. Dinner was over. Maria was not in the kitchen. Maybe she had the evening off. When Lexie saw me, she pulled out left-over pizza, salad, and chips.

"Here," she said. "We didn't wait for you, but you must be hungry. Eat."

"Thanks!" After I washed my hands, I sat, prayed quickly and began chowing down. Lexie and Brian, perched on the chairs, watched me.

Lexie was the first to speak. "Where did you go? We were worried about you."

I gulped down some milk and wiped my mouth. "When did you get back from the ball game?"

"About an hour ago." She touched my arm. "Ugh! You're wet! What happened?"

"I went for a ride on Honey. Back to the cabin. Where's your mom?"

"Mom went back into town to meet Dad. They had something important to do. Seemed kind of secretive. I wish they hadn't gone, especially with this kidnapping hanging over our heads, and both Sedge and Mr.Smithers are gone."

"Sedge is gone?" I finished off a wedge of pizza and dove into another one. Maria made the best pizza in the world.

Brian nodded. "Yeah. We saw him drive off. Probably going into town for dinner."

"Oh! That reminds me!" I hopped up from the chair and grabbed my purse from the closet, then dug my cell phone out of it. "I have to call Mr. Walters right away! I found the other sock, Lexie! Look!" I pulled the two soggy pieces of paper from my jean's pocket and laid them carefully on the counter.

Lexie and Brian read the notes while I dialed Mr. Walters. But I only got a secretary at the RCMP office. "Hello," I said as calmly as I could. My wet clothes were making me tremble. "This is Jodi Fischer. I'd like to talk to Mr. Walters, please."

She answered formally, "Yes, Jodi. He said to tell you if you called that he's busy right now. I'll leave him a voice mail. He said he'd get in touch with you as soon as he could."

"Okay. Good-bye." I snapped my phone shut and turned back to the table. Sat down and finished my pizza.

"Why didn't he answer?" Brian was bobbing around the kitchen with too much energy. "Did you tell them we have the other note? And that the kidnappers were at the cabin?"

I grimaced. "Sit down, buster, or you'll break something."

He made a face. "But where did you find this … the missing sock and the note?"

I told them everything that had happened that afternoon.

Brian pushed his mop of hair from his eyes and frowned. "But what I can't understand is why the

134

crooks put the note in the two socks in the first place. With the message all scrambled up like that."

I carried my plate and glass to the kitchen. "The way I figure is that there were two groups of them working together and the note was written to inform the group on this end of their plans. But they had to keep it secret, so they tore the note into two and put them in the socks. Only the person with both could read the note."

"And now we have the whole message!" Brian exclaimed, leaping up again. "What are we going to *do*?"

"I'm going to get into something dry," I said and hurried off to the bedroom.

I changed my clothes, then joined Lexie and Brian on the back deck. "There's something else I haven't told you about." I told them about the light I'd seen in the window of the barn and the way I felt when I went to return the bridle to the tack room. "Something stopped me." I felt again the shivers on my arms. I looked at the barn, and even now wondered if someone was watching us from there.

"Stopped you?" Lexie regarded me wide-eyed, like I just said I'd seen an alien or something.

I nodded. "I know it sounds weird, but it was like a big hand held my foot up. It stopped me from going into the barn. It was the most bizarre thing that's ever happened to me!"

"Oh, man." Lexie collapsed into the swing. "I wonder what's going on! Jodi, what do you think?"

I perched on the railing and ticked off the facts on my fingers. "One, the kidnappers left the cabin. Two, we saw that man in the woods, carrying stuff, coming this way. Three, I see a light in the window of the loft. Four, the police haven't caught the kidnappers yet – or at least, it's not on the news yet – "

"And five, you're stopped from going into the barn by something – maybe your guardian angel!" Brian bounced a basketball -- *smack!, smack!, smack!* -- on the deck.

I jumped up. "They must be *in the barn!*"

"Sh! Not so loud!" Lexie seemed frozen as she stared at it across the lawn and the pasture. "I wonder if it's true!"

I swallowed hard. Fear clamped icy hands on my heart. For a minute, I couldn't talk, couldn't even think. The sight of masked men holding guns, shoving their way into our warm home, came into my head. I gripped the top railing so hard my knuckles were white. "Let's get inside and lock the doors. Lexie, does your dad have a gun?"

"Yeah, but the cabinet's locked. I wouldn't want to shoot one of his big ones."

I tried to smile. "Neither would I."

"But why would they come to *this* barn?" Brian held the ball to his chest.

"Because the police found out their safe house, and this was handy. I bet they have a police scanner."

We went inside. Lexie locked the doors and pulled down the blinds on all the windows that faced the barn. She plunked down on a chair like her knees had given out and brushed back her hair. "Now, let's get a grip. We have to think of what to do."

I almost laughed. I knew she was scared silly, but her words were so calm and grown-up, you'd think she faced this kind of thing all the time.

A verse from the Bible came back to me – not the ones in Proverbs, but a Psalm I'd read earlier. *What time I am afraid, I will trust the Lord. The Lord is my helper, what can man do to me?* It steadied me somehow, like big powerful arms were wrapped around me.

I got a drink of water. "We don't know for sure if the gang is in the barn. We'll have to find out. Let's see. We can't leave the house by the back door, or they'll see us. We have to go out the front door, then down to the road, keeping behind those bushes. After that, we can cut across the gully, through the woods, and sneak up to the back door of the barn. There aren't any windows on that side, if I remember right."

"*We!* What's this *we* stuff?" Lexie paced the floor, her nervous energy all but tripping her as she scurried around like a trapped mouse. "Jodi, we are *not* leaving this house! I'm not, anyway. I'm staying right here!"

Brian glanced up from the game he was playing on Lexie's laptop. "We're not any safer here than outside. Jodi and me can go to the barn. Lexie can keep watch from here."

I leaned closer. "Yeah, and if you hear anything, you can whistle. Remember that whistle I taught you? Like this?" I cupped my hands together, thumbs toward my mouth, and blew through the opening, creating a soft, hooting sound.

She nodded. "I remember. But please be careful! I'll call the police if you're not back pretty soon!"

I fetched a small flashlight from my room, nodded briefly to Brian, and opened the front door. We slipped out into the rapidly falling darkness. I heard Lexie take a position near the front door in the bushes. I led the way, hunched over like I'd seen them do in movies, across the front lawn to the hedge that lined the driveway.

"I'm glad it's dark," Brian whispered as we crept forward slowly.

"Yeah, me too. Let's get through these bushes and go over to those woods. If we can make it there, we'll be okay."

"I'm right behind you."

It's funny to say, but once we were out and doing something, I didn't feel nearly so terrified. And Brian's remark sounded so much like what you'd hear in a movie, I almost laughed out loud. But I didn't.

The grass was wet and pretty soon my second pair of jeans were soaked! We got across the driveway, through a barbed wire fence, and made it to the woods. I tried not to step on twigs or make unnecessary noises as we crawled through the fence and approached the barn. My heart hammered in my ears, and I found it hard to take a breath.

I gripped Brian's arm and drew him close. "We have to go really slow now. I'll go first and when we reach the barn, you stay *right* behind me."

"Roger-doger, *moi capitaine*."

I knew he was trying to be funny, but it wasn't a joke anymore. Probably a band of desperate criminals was hiding in the barn with a baby they'd kidnapped. What would stop them from taking one of us – or killing us? I know it's a gruesome thought, but it happens. It happens all the time.

We started out again, creeping along slowly, trying to keep in cover. An owl hooted up in the big pine tree and the cows lowed softly to their babies. A big moon came out – I wished it had been overcast!

We got to the barn. I leaned against the solid wood planking and took a deep breath. So far so good! Now came the worst part – sneaking up to the rear door and looking in. What would we see? Well, there was only one way to find out …

Slowly I crept along the wall, taking each step with great care. One false move now and it would be over! I was aware that the horses were standing near the water tank in the corner of the corral and that Honey was looking at me. I prayed she wouldn't come over to see what I was doing in hopes of a treat! I thought maybe if she started my way, I'd grab that rope that was hanging on a fence post and tie her away from me. She had a halter on.

I turned my head and tried to focus on the job. We knelt on the very doorstep of the barn door and stared into the long wide center aisle, holding our breath like we were diving into a pool. It sorta felt like that, too.

That's when I heard it. A board screeched. I grabbed Brian's arm and saw his eyes widen and felt his body stiffen.

It felt like someone was stuffing my head in a pillow. I let my breath out and took another one. *Breathe. Just breathe!* It was dark in the barn, but from the other end of the aisle enough light streamed in so I could see. Nothing was there, except the usual –

the center hall, stalls doors, a bale of hay near the door.

I leaned back and pulled Brian with me. We sat there, staring into the darkness.

"What're we going to do?" Brian whispered, pulling at blades of grass.

"I don't know!" All we had to go on was that one screech of a board. Not enough to call Mr. Walters and have the police come charging out here.

"Well, I'm not going to sit here and get my butt wet." He hoisted himself up to his knees, then stood.

"What are you doing?"

"I'm going in there."

"No! Brian, no!" I couldn't holler, but my whisper was as stern as I could make it. He didn't listen to me. He never listens to me. I tried to grab him, but he was too fast. He slipped past my fingers and went into the barn!

I scrambled to my feet. "Brian! Come back!" But he was gone – creeping slowly down the center aisle to the far end where a stair led to the loft. I chewed my fingernails and paced back and forth, wondering what I should do. If I went in, there would be no one left to get help. But how could I just stand out here and allow
–

There was a scuffling sound, thudding footsteps, and a screech that raised the hair on the back of my neck.

"Hey!" It was Brian. "Let me go! Get your hands –
" A heavy *thud!*

Now I could make out what was happening. A man's dark shadow seemed to fill most of the open space. He was holding onto … *Brian!* And Brian was not making it easy. With a sickening of my stomach, I knew the man had hit him. Now he was dragging Brian up the aisle toward the stairs. Would he kidnap my brother, too?

Suddenly a red wave flooded my mind. *No way!* I slammed my fist into the barn wall. *Ouch!* The pain brought me to my senses. Hitting the barn wasn't going to help Brian. I looked around frantically. *Honey. The rope on the fence.*

I leaped to the fence, grabbed the rope and dashed to the horses. Honey shied away from my rapid advance. I stopped, called to her softly. She whinnied, a low sound in her throat, and came to me. I looped the rope through her halter under her neck and leaped up on her, taking both ends of the rope in my hands and using them like reins.

She seemed to sense my urgency, for she responded immediately when I kicked her. By the time we reached the barn door, she was going at a pretty fast clip. I knew I had only a few seconds of surprise to do what I had to do, and so I didn't pull back on the rope at all as she lunged into the barn and clomped heavily down the center aisle.

Somewhere in the back of my mind I heard someone yell. To this day, I don't know who it was, but I'm thinking it was Brian. It all happened so fast, I didn't have time to be scared of the man standing there, holding Brian's arm in a death grip, or of the gun that he brought up—like in slow motion.

I saw the metal of the gun barrel glint in the moonlight. I saw his eyes – evil eyes, and I knew he intended to shoot me. Kill me. Then Brian. I kicked Honey and felt her charge forward. Right at that man. His eyes widened just before she struck him with her shoulder. He went flying, his gun with him.

"Brian! C'mon!" I screamed at him, then rode on out into the moonlight. I pulled on the rope sharply and Honey slid to a stop. I turned her. Brian bolted from the barn door like a cat on fire.

I kicked Honey and headed back for him. He reached up. Grabbing his arm, I pulled him up behind me. It was so smooth, like we'd practiced it all our lives. Yet I'd never tried to yank someone from the ground and seat him on a running horse before, and I'm sure Brian never tried that trick, either.

But there he was, safe behind me. I turned Honey and we raced to the other end of the pasture. We both slid off at the same time and landed in a heap on the grass. I leaped up, pulled the rope from Honey's halter, patted her, and sent her back to the other horses. She seemed glad to go.

"Well, that was something!" My knees shook, my teeth chattered, my heart was pounding in my ears, but I tried to look calm. I pulled him to his feet and hugged him. "You okay?"

"Yeah. Thanks, Jodi." His arms encircled my waist and I swear he was crying. "I'll ... never ... *ever* fight with you ... again. Ever."

I laughed, tears streaming down my cheeks, too. "You know, sometimes I holler at you, but you're the best thing that's ever happened to me!" We snuffled together for awhile and then he dropped his arms like he was embarrassed.

"Well, I guess we found out that they're in the barn. Now what?"

I grinned. Leave it to him to be two steps ahead of me! "We gotta get back to Lexie and warn her! They might come up to the house and try something, now that they know we know they're there! C'mon!" I took off running and figured he'd keep up.

He didn't just keep up. He passed me.

CHAPTER THIRTEEN

Another Surprise

"We've got to call the police!" I shouted, heedless of the danger now, as we drew near the house. I saw Lexie's figure emerge from the shadows of the bushes.

She opened the door and I flew into the house after Brian. Lexie locked the door and stared at us like she'd never seen us before. "What happened?"

"There was a man in the barn. He caught Brian and hit him! Then I rode in on Honey and she … slammed into him, and I grabbed Brian and we got out of there."

"Yeah. You should've seen her, Lexie! I mean, it was *awesome!* Like the best rescue ever! Better than the movies, cuz we were *doing* it!"

I told her, in more understandable language, what happened.

She led the way to the kitchen. It seems no matter what, you always go to the kitchen for comfort. She fell into a chair. "That's awful! They must have the baby, then!"

I grabbed my phone and dialed 911. The dispatcher answered and asked what my problem was. I told her as calmly as I could, but I was crying before I got it all out and she was saying, "Don't hang up. Stay with me. I'm getting someone out there. Now, where are you?"

I told her as best as I could and had Lexie give some more details. By then, she said Mr. Walters was on the line. Man, it was good to hear his voice! I told him everything that had happened. "So they must have the baby up there in the loft, Mr. Walters! And now they might come over here to the house! Would you please hurry and come?"

"Okay. I'm on my way. Why don't you three kids go out the front door and make your way to the road? I'll be along in a few minutes. Just keep to the shadows and if you see anyone, hunker down and don't make a sound, okay?"

I swallowed. "Okay."

Out on the road again, we walked away from the house about a quarter of a mile. Then we sat down. The moon shone brightly, almost like daylight, but it was a silvery kind of light that bathed the fields and trees and pastures in an unworldly light. Like we'd stepped out onto another planet or into another world. Maybe it was Narnia!

But, no, this was real -- sitting beside the road in the dark, waiting for Mr. Walters. I hugged my knees to my chest and tried to keep my tone light for Brian's sake. "I wonder what's taking him so long."

Brian tossed a rock across the road. "It always seems long when you have to wait."

Lexie sat upright suddenly. "I just had a horrible thought! What if they're listening on their police scanner and they send their other gang to get us! What if they get here before the police do?"

I shrugged, but fear squeezed my heart again. Had we escaped one danger to put ourselves in another?

145

And what if Mr. Walters was paid off by the crooks? We'd be sitting ducks out here.

"I can't stand this," I said. "Let's run over to the woods on the other side of the road and hide." They didn't say anything. I held my breath and listened. Was that a motor?

Brian stood up, listening, too. The sound grew louder.

"Here they come!" I scrambled to my feet. Down the road I could make out the dark shapes of cars, creeping along with their lights off.

The cars pulled up alongside us and four RCMP officers climbed out. A fifth man walked over to us. It was Mr. Walters! Breathlessly, almost all at once, we filled him in on the details. It didn't take more than a few moments. After that, the constables moved off into the darkness, creeping toward the barn.

Mr. Walters fixed his eyes on the barn. "You kids get inside the house. Lock the doors and stay down on the floor." He hurried off.

"Oh, th-this is so sc-scary," I stuttered as we slipped into the house. My teeth chattered; it felt like winter all over again, I was so cold. After Lexie made sure all the doors were locked and the curtains drawn, we huddled in the kitchen on the tile floor. I pulled my little flashlight from my pocket and turned it on, shielding the light with my hand.

"I wish we could watch!" Lexie breathed.

Brian sighed. "Well, we can't. Hey, go get your cards, Lexie. We can start a game of flinch or something."

"Now?" She stared at him.

He shrugged. "Why not?"

I hugged myself and shook my head. "Do…n't th…think I c…could concentrate." I seemed to be okay when I was doing something, but this waiting in the dark was getting to me. I could imagine the officers creeping up to the barn, up those stairs to the loft … and then what? Would the kidnappers kill the baby?

Suddenly I heard a shot! "Oh, no!" I started to jump up and run to the window, but Lexie pulled me back.

"He said to stay down!"

"I wonder what's happened!" Brian squirmed impatiently.

"Couldn't we just crawl over to the door and open it a teensy bit?" I was already on my knees. Brian was ready to join me and Lexie reluctantly followed.

"This is silly," she grumbled.

"It isn't nearly as silly as being shot at through the window." I reached the door and opened it just a crack.

Suddenly the door flew inward. Someone screamed and someone else yelled. I toppled back and somebody, somebody very heavy, landed on me. We were all in a heap. I pulled myself free and shone the light on the person who'd come barging in the door, afraid it was the crooks.

It was one of the constables! He managed to stand up.

"Oh, it's you!" I switched on the light as Lexie and Brian untangled themselves and got to their feet. "What's going on? Have they captured the crooks?"

"And did they save the baby?" Lexie pushed back her hair. We all looked more than a little messy, but the constable, a young man with a big smile and blue eyes, didn't seem to mind.

He holstered his gun. "I thought you'd like to know – they have three of the kidnappers. They also got the baby safely away from them." He glanced back over his shoulder at the sound of heavy footsteps on the deck. "Oh, it's Mr. Walters. He'll fill you in on the details."

I rushed outside, almost into Mr. Walter's arms. The constables had their squad car lights going and in the swirling red and blue, I saw three figures lined up against the corral fence. One of them was a woman. Then I spotted another one, being led forward. He was smaller than the others, skinny and tall. Colton!

I shook my head, all the fear and repulsion I'd felt for that guy draining out of me like water from a leaky bucket. In its place, I felt only sadness for him.

"The case is solved!" Mr. Walters said with a big smile. "Colton was their local contact. That woman, by the way, is the one I spoke to at the cabin that day."

"What about the baby? Matthew Salisbury? Is he going to be all right?" Lexie surged forward, her face pale in the porch light. "How come we never heard him crying or anything?"

He removed his hat, smoothed down his hair, and returned his hat to his head. "Well, the baby isn't in too good of condition, I'm afraid to say." Just then an ambulance arrived with siren wailing and lights blazing. "They'll take him in to the hospital. I hope they can save him."

"You … mean, he's about gone?"

Mr. Walters sighed. I could see he was really tired. "They must have kept him sedated with drugs. This is all connected with drugs, I'm afraid. He's suffering from exposure, too, I imagine. But we hope – "

"And pray!" I finished for him.

One of the squad cars pulled out of the driveway. I watched them go, feeling a little funny in the pit of my stomach.

"Hey! Who is *that?*" Brian pointed to another car that was approaching the house.

I watched it come closer. And closer. Was it the Marshals? No. Then suddenly I knew. "It's Mom and Dad!" I rushed over to the car just as Dad, his whole tall, smiling, sandy-haired self, emerged from the car. I fell into his arms. That's when I really started crying!

"Jodi!" He held me tightly and opened his arms further for the onslaught of Brian coming to greet him. "What – Brian! What's going on here?"

"Oh, Dad! I'm so glad you're home!" I couldn't get anything else out of my mouth.

From the other side of the car, Mom came running. Her wavy, brown hair fell around her shoulders and her usually sunny blue eyes were dark with worry. She grabbed me and Brian both, holding us like she'd never let us go.

"Jodi! Brian! What in the world – why are all these officers here? Are you okay?"

I leaned on her for a second, relief flooding my heart like a dam that's broken. I introduced Mr. Walters to them.

"Glad to meet you," the detective said, shaking their hands in turn. "We have things under control now. Part of a gang of criminals was holed up in a cabin not far from here. They had kidnapped a baby. The kids here got suspicious first and told us about it. But we got sidetracked. I think they tried to decoy us away tonight while they made their escape. But anyway, Jodi found the missing clue and discovered that they'd moved to the barn." More police cars left.

Mom's arm tightened around my waist. "You mean there were *kidnappers* right here?" She glanced around uneasily as if they would jump out and steal us from her grip.

"Yeah, Mom," Brian piped up, escaping her arms. "It was almost like on TV! Except maybe a little scarier. And you should have seen Jodi! She saved me from them! She rode that guy down and he had to drop me!"

"What's this?" Mr. Walters turned to me, surprised.

"Oh, uh. Nothing much, sir." I shuffled my feet, hoping he wouldn't ask more questions.

"I can make some coffee, Mrs. Fischer, if you'd like some." Lexie pressed forward and was rewarded by a big hug from Mom. Then she glanced at the detective. "You, too, Mr. Walters. And I bet I can find some of Marie's famous cinnamon rolls."

Mr. Walters looked a little tempted, but then shook his head. "I should contact the parents." He glanced up to the porch. "But I guess a cup of coffee would be okay, Lexie. C'mon, Jodi, you can help me."

I was surprised he said that, but the party moved into the house which was now brilliantly lit. Marie had come back some time in the midst of all the excitement and she had coffee already made.

Mr. Walters drew out his phone and dialed the number. "Hello? Who am I speaking to? This is Mr. Walters, detective for the RCMP in Quesnel. Yes … yes. I have news for you concerning Matthew. Yes. Good news. He is safe and sound this very minute, on his way to the hospital …"

He held the phone out so I could hear the shouting, laughing, crying.

Lexie was beside me. We hugged each other. I felt like I was bursting with happiness.

Mr. Walters spoke again in the phone. "We captured the gang and have them in custody. I want you to know that most of the credit for this happy ending is due to two girls." He briefly told them how Lexie and I had helped solve the case. When he finished, he glanced at me. "Sure. Here she is." He handed me the phone. "They want to thank you."

I was so surprised and confused, I almost dropped it. I held it so Lexie could hear, too. "Hello? This is Jodi Fischer."

A man's strong voice, heavy with an English accent, and husky with emotion, answered. "Jodi, I understand you were responsible for saving my son's life – " He stopped and cleared his throat.

"I'm just so glad we could help," I said. "And … I have to say that God helped me do it. I was so scared, but I prayed hard and He helped me."

"We've been doing a lot of that recently, too," he replied. "We want you to know how much we appreciate what you've done. My wife and I thank you from the bottom of our hearts."

Tears came again – *darn!* My heart was filled with gratefulness and gladness, so much so that I could hardly tell him good-bye. I handed the phone back to Mr. Walters and he finished the conversation.

Mom brought Mr. Walters a cup of coffee. After he gulped it down, we walked with him to his car. Mom put her arm around Lexie. "Where are your folks?" We waved Mr. Walters good-bye.

Lexie smiled, but I sensed she was very sad and lonely. "Oh, they'll be here soon. They went somewhere tonight. They wouldn't tell me. Have you had supper? Marie can round you up something, you know."

Mom laughed. "No, I have two girls asleep in the car, so we better get home. Jodi, can you gather up your things, or do you want to stay the night and come home tomorrow?"

"I think I'll stay, Mom. My things are pretty scattered and Brian's stuff is even worse." I glanced up as another car came in the driveway. "Hey, look! Lexie, your folks are back!"

A smile flooded her face. "Oh, yeah! Just wait until they hear what's been going on!" She started over to the car but I could tell she was puzzled by their behavior. They didn't jump out and come running over to us.

It seemed they were taking a long time to get out of the car. Mr. Marshal walked around and opened the door for Traci. Even then they didn't look up or greet their daughter. Then Mr. Marshal opened the back door and they seemed to rummage around in the back seat for awhile.

Lexie stood not far from them, her hands on his hips, waiting. I knew she was bursting with her news. I knew she wanted to run into their arms like I had with my folks. I knew tears were even now brimming in her brown eyes. I took a step forward, but Mom caught my arm and shook her head.

Mr. Marshal lifted something from the back seat and placed it in Traci's arms.

"What does he have?" I craned my neck to see.

Lexie gave a little strangled cry. I dashed over to her.

"Mom! Dad! What – " She stopped, stock still. I almost crashed into her. Traci turned, a big smile on her face. I'd never seen her so happy before. She was holding a small bundle, wrapped in a blue blanket.

"Sh! I think he's asleep!" She unfolded a corner of the blanket and there, sleeping like a little angel, was Mark! "He's *ours*, Lexie," she whispered. "*Yours!*"

I thought Lexie was going to faint. She was so still, almost like a wax figure, standing there with the bright moonlight on her face, staring at her new baby brother. She looked at her Mom, then her Dad. She was speechless, but tears poured down her cheeks and her shining face told the whole story.

Very tenderly Traci placed the child in her arms.

CHAPTER FOURTEEN

No More Secrets

"Oh! Jodi, look, isn't he's beautiful?" Lexie couldn't take her eyes from the sweet face wrapped in the blue blanket. "How ... what can I say? Wow. This is better than Christmas."

We all laughed.

But I was confused. "What's Mark doing here?"

Traci smiled at me. "We'd like to introduce our new son to you. Mark Marshal. I have to admit, I'm surprised, too."

My mom gave her a hug, and Dad shook Mr. Marshal's hand.

Mr. Marshal almost looked embarrassed. "We've been working on the process for over two years, and tonight we got the word."

Traci giggled. "Like I said, I was totally unprepared. I think I'm going to have to do some major shopping tomorrow. Want to come along, Patty?"

"I'm up for it." Mom shot a glance at me, as if she wanted to include me in the trip. I gave my head a tiny nod.

"Well, let's get inside," Traci said, nudging Lexie to the door. "We should get him to bed. Then we can have some coffee."

Dad grinned. "Yes. And we have to get these girls to tell us their story. When we arrived, an ambulance was just leaving, and the yard was full of RCMP constables!"

Traci gasped. "An ambulance! Police! Lexie, what's happened?"

"It's okay now, Mom. Honest! We'll tell you the whole story in just a minute."

"Yeah, and I have some questions, too." I held the door for Lexie as she carried the baby into the house.

About that time, the twins woke up. Mom went and got them from the car. They were sleepy-eyed and tousled, but I gave them a hug. It was good to see them. We found a place for Mark in the Marshal's bedroom. Traci brought out two beautiful, soft blankets and made him a bed on the floor.

After we got him settled, we went to the living room. Mr. Marshal turned on the gas fireplace and Marie came in with a tray, loaded with coffee and cocoa.

I snuggled down by Dad on the couch. He put his arm around me.

"Now, Jodi. Don't keep us in suspense any longer."

I cleared my throat and straightened. "I ... I hardly know where to begin." I glanced at Brian on the stool by the fire and Lexie who sprawled on the rug with a cushion under her head.

"I guess it all began the day Cheyenne ran away in the woods and we found a wallet."

I told the story, interrupted now and then by comments from Lexie and Brian. When I related the threatening phone call and the strange man at the door, Mr. Marshal shook his head.

"I'm really sorry I didn't take you girls more seriously," he said. "I just thought it was some pranksters around here. I guess that will teach me a lesson to pay more attention to my family. And less to my business." He looked so shamefaced that I felt sorry for him. That's when I started to like him.

I told about how Brian and I crept up to the barn, but I kind of skimmed over the part I played in freeing Brian from the kidnappers. But I didn't get away with it.

He took the floor, standing up in his excitement, and blabbed it all in great detail. Little bugger! I noticed Mr. Marshal making a note in the small book he carried in his pocket, and I hoped so hard that he wasn't going to call the newspaper about it!

Traci couldn't get over it. She kept exclaiming over and over, "If I'd just known!" And, "But it was so dangerous! You could've been killed!"

Lexie grasped her hand tightly. "Don't worry about it, Mom. Everything turned out all right and God was watching over us. I wish you'd trust in Him, like I do. He was taking care of us."

I nodded in full agreement. "She's right. I was so scared most of the time, I couldn't think straight. But the Lord helped me. I just wish I wasn't such a coward and had more courage."

"Jodi," Dad said softly, "courage isn't the absence of fear. Courage is doing what you know is right and trusting God for the rest. I think you're very courageous. And I'm proud of you."

"Thanks, Dad." I gave him a one-armed hug and turned back to the group. "I'm still wondering … about the Clarks, those people who brought Mark here. That sure confused me. I thought …" I didn't want to say out loud what I thought, but Mr. Marshal saved me from having to explain.

He chuckled. "I'm sorry about that, Jodi. And you, too, Lexie. You see, Traci and I have wanted to adopt a child for a long time and when the daughter of a friend of ours had Mark, but didn't want him, I started looking into it right away. The deal was going along really well, so I decided to see if Lexie would take to him or not. So I paid an employer of mine and his wife to bring Mark up here for a weekend."

"Whew! That explains a lot!" I sank back on the couch.

Mr. Marshal continued, "I've been spending too much time away from home. I've thought about it a lot, and I've decided to drop out of politics."

There was a general lifting of spirits in the room. Traci even clapped her hands and said, "Oh, good!" Lexie moved to the chair and sat on his lap. "Oh, Dad, I'm so glad!"

"I think it's about time we went home," Mom said, indicating the two little girls asleep in front of the fire. "These kids have had a big day."

We let the grown-ups say their good-byes and went to the bedroom.

Lexie plopped down on her bed with a happy sigh. "Oh, Jodi! I think you're so cool! And I'm so glad I'm your best friend!"

I laughed and caught a glimpse of my twinkling blue eyes and frouzy reddish brown hair in the mirror. "Well, thanks, but I'm just plain old Jodi Fischer, the girl who's forever embarrassing you. And it was God who helped us through it all. Don't forget that!"

She laughed. "Don't worry. I won't.'

Just before we turned out the light, we decided to have another peek at Mark, so we tiptoed into the Marshal's bedroom. After we gazed at his sweet form lying so still on the floor, we decided we needed a drink. But my folks hadn't left yet. The four grown-ups were still in the kitchen, talking.

We drew closer.

Mr. Marshal was saying, "Well, we haven't said anything to Lexie yet, but we'd like to move up here permanently."

I clasped Lexie in a hug. Then I put my finger to my lips.

Traci said, "Yeah, we like the country, and the neighbors. And it's a lot better place to raise Mark and Lexie." There was a pause, then she continued in a lower voice, "We'd really like to go to church with you sometime, too. I guess I've thought that having a baby would solve all our problems, but now that I have one, I know we'd better raise him right."

Mom spoke up. "Oh, Traci, that's great! Why don't you come next Sunday and we'll have a barbeque." There was some more grown-up talk, but we didn't want to hear it.

We stood there in the hall in our pajamas and hugged each other. Then creeping to the bedroom, we quietly shut the door.

ABOUT THE AUTHOR

Virginia Ann Work lives in eastern Washington State with her husband and her cat. On any given day you might find her writing on her computer, taking a walk through the woods, or talking to one of her three grown children or five grand-children. She is the wife of a busy pastor, so she has many things to do in the church.

She loves horses, is an artist with acrylics and chalk, and loves to travel, swim, and ride bikes. She wrote the original Jodi Mystery Series in 1980-1985 and had them published by Moody Press. At that time she was the wife of a missionary pastor in a small town in British Columbia, had three small children, and wrote on typewriter. Having the five Jodi books published was a dream come true for her.

But the dream ended sooner than she wanted. In 1988, Moody Press wrote her a letter, saying they no longer wanted to publish the series. She went on to write many other stories, but always wanted to see the Jodi Mystery Series back in print. She has received letters from teens from all around the world who said how much they enjoyed the stories about Jodi and her friends.

Now, twenty-three years later, she rewrote the original book and would like to get all the five Jodi books in print and on ebooks. She would also like to write more of them!

Check out her other novels at her website, http://www.virginiaawork.com and come back to see what other books she has. The next book in print will be **Jodi: The Secret in the Silver Box**. For a sneak preview, read on.

Preview of Jodi: The Secret in the Silver Box:

Prologue

Okay, I know. I bet you think I'm getting stuck on myself, writing another story, and how could anything get more exciting than the mystery with the Salisbury baby? It turns out that I'm sort of like a magnet, attracting all sorts of adventures, and when I had another one that same summer, I thought I should write about it, too. Mom says I better stop having these ... incidents, as she calls them ... or else I won't grow up and give her any grandchildren. It sounds like something a mom would say, doesn't it?

So here I am again. Jodi E. Fischer, your ordinary teenager, going into the tenth grade, best friend of Lexie Marshal, proud owner of Honey, the amazing horse who won best of class at the horse show last week. Or does she own me? It's a toss-up. Some days I swear that she thinks she's the boss.

Well, this time we're off to the gold mining days of British Columbia's historic 1860's. Hang onto your seats, cuz this one's a bumpy ride. I promise you won't be bored.

Chapter One

A Mysterious Stranger

Shivers chased up and down my arms as I stood alone in the middle of the road and stared at an old log cabin in the center of a small meadow.

Sugar, my white terrier, sniffed the ground around my feet. She didn't like the way I wasn't going anywhere. She scented a dozen smells from the forest she would've liked to explore, and so she tugged on the leash and whined.

A crow cawed from the top of a towering pine, and something told me I should turn around right then and head back to our campsite. But of course I hardly ever listen to those thoughts, and this time was no different.

I was curious. Up on the wide porch, I spotted an old man in a rocking chair. Was he a dummy, like I'd seen in the restored buildings in downtown Barkerville? But then he moved. I almost swallowed my gum. The voice urging me to turn and run was louder than ever.

Sugar spotted him about the same time I did and she barked, then ran and hid behind my legs. The little coward. Who was the old man? Maybe he was a real live prospector. Now wouldn't that be something? I could tell Lexie I'd met one of the old-timers who'd started Barkerville.

But maybe I'd better start at the beginning. Let's rewind to this morning, the day that the Fischer family had been looking forward to forever.

It dawned bright and sunny with a deep cobalt blue sky and not a cloud in sight. A whole week of vacation stretched out in front of us; it would be great, I just knew it. We were all excited, but I don't think Brian, my ten-year-old brother, had slept for two nights, he was so wound up.

To top things off, our neighbors, the Marshals, loaned us their motor home, which was one of those super-deluxe models with pull-outs and soft carpets and a flat screen TV and a microwave and everything. After we spent a day in Barkerville, we planned to drive over to the campground at Bowron Lakes where my Uncle Ron and my cousin Stephen were meeting us. In the morning, the guys were going to take off on a four-day canoeing trip around the lakes, while the girls swam and sun bathed and watched movies. Mom brought her laptop and wanted to finish the book she was writing. What made the trip even more fun was the fact that I'd persuaded Lexie to join us.

We arrived in Barkerville just before lunch, and after a quick bite, we set off to explore it, leaving Sugar to guard our campsite. It's funny to say, but even though we'd lived near Quesnel for ten years, we'd never been to see the old town. When we got back to the campsite about two hours later, Brian and Dad made an emergency trip to Wells to buy some matches, which they'd forgotten, despite many lists.

That's when I decided to take the dog for a walk. I got up from the lawn chair and stretched. "I'm going to take Sugar for a little stroll around town," I said, fastening on her leash. "You wanta come, Lexie?"

Lexie shook her head and got a book from her bag. "No thanks." She settled on a lawn chair.

Mom plunked into another one with her laptop. "Just stay out of trouble, Jodi. If you can. And don't be gone too long."

That's just like Mom. She never trusts me. "I won't. I promise."

"Can I come?" Bethany emerged from the motor home and gazed at me with big pleading eyes.

"Yeah, me too!" Brittany was right behind her.

My five-year-old twin sisters were cute, and everyone *oohes* and *aahes* over them, but sometimes they can be pests. Right now I wanted to be alone. "Not this time," I said, turning away and striding out of the parking lot, getting pulled forward by Sugar's eager pace. I knew they were standing there, side by side, a disappointed look on both their faces, and I knew that if I glanced back at them I'd relent and wave them to come with me.

I wanted to think about Randy Abbot. Yesterday after church, he'd actually *noticed* me. I was standing by the door, waiting for Mom and Dad to get done talking, and he came up, like he was going outside, then he stops and says hi. At first it was just polite talk, but then he asked if we needed help at the bake sale the youth group is doing and we got to laughing, because I said, yeah, you can bake some cookies.

He offered to help set up tables and check back every so often with water.

Wow. I couldn't believe it. He's *so cute,* and he's nice, too. Kind of quiet, especially around girls, which is maybe why he doesn't pay much attention to me.

He's a senior and a star basketball player. He's in the drama club at school, volunteers to work in camps and almost everything else they needs volunteers for, and keeps up a straight A average. Busy guy, which sorta leaves me in the dust. At least he doesn't have a girlfriend. I spend a lot of time doodling his initials -- *RA* -- in my notebook when I'm supposed to be doing homework.

A lot of girls would like to be his girlfriend. Just thinking about how they talk about him made me walk faster, and I'd gotten through the whole town before I knew it. Now I was in the Chinese section – evidently there'd been a lot of Chinese here at one time. I came to the end of the street, which petered out into a small lane that ran off into the woods. I followed it, not thinking much, just wondering what was down this road.

Mom always said my curiosity got me into trouble, but I didn't see the harm in trying to find out what was beyond the turn of the road.

After I'd walked for about fifteen minutes down the tiny road, I stopped, feeling strangely afraid, and glanced around uneasily. The late afternoon sun burned the top of my head. Tall trees, mostly pines and firs, surrounded me. The sapphire sky was like a dome above my head. But it was quiet – too quiet. The forest seemed to hold its breath and watch me. Sugar whined and tugged on the leash.

I wiped sweat from my forehead, and thought maybe I should go back. I could still see the tops of the tall buildings that formed the main part of the town. I'd read up on the place before we came – Billy Barker struck a huge vein of gold in 1862 and the town sprang up like magic around his dig. The strike brought hordes of men. I could almost hear gun fights on Main Street and see men bringing their sacks of gold on horseback to the assayer's office.

It must have been a noisy place then, but now it was silent – dead silent. The jitters started in my legs and worked their way up my back. Maybe I should go get Lexie. But how silly is that! Like I couldn't walk down here by myself? I'm fifteen, going on sixteen, for gosh sake.

Maybe I'd angered the gods of this place. I had to giggle. But, seriously, maybe there *were* ghosts around here. *Naw.* I shoved back my hair and shook off the shivers. I wasn't about to let a bunch of old ghosts scare me! I'd show them I wasn't afraid.

Like I was strolling through the park, I meandered down the lane, my ears pricked, my senses sharpened, shivers still racing up and down my arms. I rounded a corner and stopped.

The trees swept back from a small meadow. Front and center stood a small log cabin. And in front of the cabin, a bright yellow Volkswagon was parked. I tried not to stare at the old man who sat so still on the porch.

He saw me and stood, then jumped down the steps and strode toward me. I was surprised that he was so nimble, except he favored his left leg. I took a step back as he approached, keeping a safe distance between us. Sugar wanted to go and greet him. Some guardian dog! My next dog is definitely going to be a German Shepherd.

"Howdy, miss." His blue eyes twinkled with fun and a smile creased his weathered face. He wore patched flannel pants held up with suspenders and a red plaid shirt. As he drew near, I smelled tobacco and wood smoke. He bent and patted Sugar who groveled at his feet, all wiggles and licks. "Cute dog."

"Her name's Sugar."

"I owned a terrier once." He straightened. "Best dog I ever had. Didn't have a packrat on the place the whole time." He grinned and held out his hand. "Name's Joe McCallahan, miss."

I shook his hand gingerly. "I'm Jodi Fischer, sir." I chuckled nervously. "I thought you were one of those manikins. But you're real. Which is a relief." What a stupid thing to say, but I was still unsure of him and it made me blurt out any old thing.

He hitched up his pants. "Come on up t'the porch, Jodi, and talk for a spell. Not every day a pretty girl and her pup comes callin'. I'm kinda lonesome back in here, even though the town's just a spit and holler away." He grinned, revealing yellowed teeth.

I didn't like the word *spell,* but my curiosity got the better of me. "Are … are you a prospector, Mr. McCallahan?" I knew I should politely tell him goodbye and get back to our camp site, but he didn't seem to be dangerous and I knew I could run faster than him, even if he was spry.

"Call me Joe, miss. They call me Sucker Joe, cuz I never struck it rich."

I followed him to the bottom of the steps. "I better be getting back, Mr. Joe." I was going to turn and walk away, but I hesitated. How could I pass up a chance to talk to a real prospector? I wondered if he knew Billy Barker, then dismissed that idea immediately. No, that was over a hundred and fifty years ago. But maybe his father had known him.

"Come on up. Sit awhile." He favored his left leg as he climbed the steps to the porch and settled in a wicker rocking chair. A coffee cup and newspapers were on a table beside the chair. He pierced me with a blue-eyed glance and grinned. "I won't hurt you. Heck, I wouldn't hurt a flea, and that there's the gol-darned truth."

He sure talked funny. It intrigued me. I perched on the top step of the porch, scratching Sugar around her ears. Silence settled down around us. He seemed content with it, but my heart was pounding in my ears, almost like I knew something lurked in the dark shadows of the forest, something that watched with hungry intent.

Finally I said, "Do you live in Quesnel, Mr. Joe?"

He wiped his mouth. "Nope. I live down by McLeese Lake. I come up every summer and pan a little gold from the crick. Never find much, mind you, but a fellar never knows. Might strike a rich lode like old Mr. Barker did back in '62." He dug in his shirt pocket and pulled out a little tin box and a paper. He tapped the box to let a thin stream of dark brown stuff fall on the paper. Then he rolled it and licked it.

"Don't mind if I have a smoke, do you?" He bobbed his head.

"Oh, no. Go ahead."

He lit a match to the cigarette, took a deep puff, then leaned back and gazed over the treetops. "My gran-pappy built this here cabin back when Barkerville was just a baby town, before there was a school or a church or even the board walk. He and his brother struck gold on the crick just over there aways." He motioned vaguely through the woods. "What's your name, missy?"

I'd told him just a few moments ago, but old folks are like that. Grandpa was always forgetting stuff we'd just told him. "Jodi Fischer, sir. We live down by Quesnel. My folks are missionaries to the Indian people. We came to see the town, then we're going to camp at Bowron Lakes."

Even as the words came out of my mouth, I wanted to call them back. Why was I blurting all this information out to a total stranger? But the words were gone. I watched him carefully from the corner of my eye and saw he didn't react at all. I breathed deeply and thanked God. "Tell me about prospecting. I bet it was exciting to get gold from the stream like you did!"

"Come on in and let me show you somethin'," he said, standing. "I won't hurt you. I promise."

I knew I shouldn't do it, but again, I was curious. I followed him into the cabin, surprised it was as neat as a pin. I don't know how neat pins are, but the cabin was clean, and even the dishes were washed and draining beside the sink. It looked like he'd been fixing his lunch, because a can of Spam was on the counter, opened.

He saw where I was looking and chuckled. "Just makin' my lunch. You wouldn't like a sandwich, would you?"

"No thanks."

He showed me some pictures of his father and the claim he worked, and also some gold nuggets he kept. He said he could sell them, but he'd rather have the memories. We went back out onto the porch.

"So, I bet you made a lot a money from your claim," I said more to make conversation than out of real interest.

I expected his happy little chuckle to come again, but I was wrong. He plunked down in his rocking chair and looked down at the worn boards. He sighed. "I wouldn't know about that, miss. I've tried all my life to be as good as my pappy and my grand-pappy, but I ain't. I'd like to have a lot of money and give it to some charity and be known as a good man. But I guess I'm no good." He sighed again, a heavy sigh that seemed to contain all the sorrow in the world.

I didn't know what to say. I wanted to comfort him and lift his spirits, but I knew all too well how it felt to be a failure. A nobody. A nothing. Someone that a guy like Randy hardly even noticed. I swallowed and tried to smile. "That's not true. I'm sure you're a real nice person and you've done lots of good things."

Joe straightened. His eyes met mine for a long time, then he leaned back and puffed on his dwindling cigarette again. He didn't say anything for awhile. It was like he was pondering something real deep and I wondered what it was.

Finally he extinguished his smoke on a little tin tray. A worried expression haunted his eyes, but he managed a smile for me. "I need you to do somethin' for me, girl. It's ... strange you came along when you did, cuz I was thinkin' real hard about gettin' someone to do it fer me."

"What?" I wasn't sure about Joe, and I wasn't sure I wanted to get involved with his life or his problems. I sat there, staring at him, wondering what I should do, thinking, *yeah, now's a good time to tell him I have to go.*

I stood up and dusted off the seat of my pants. But I couldn't say the words.

The Mystery of the Missing Message

The Mystery of the Missing Message

The Mystery of the Missing Message

Virginia Ann Work

The Mystery of the Missing Message

Made in the USA
Monee, IL
13 August 2021

75281131R00105